Guardian of the Monarch Moon

A Novel

by

D. S. Cuellar

壱

弐

Guardian of the Monarch Moon

Visit us on Facebook at
Guardian of the Red Butterfly

Cover Design by Roslyn McFarland

参

Special Thanks to:

Editor:
Pauline Suite

Technical Support:
Ryan Wintersteen

And a special thanks to David Morrell for his encouragement and correspondence.

四

Candy —

The next adventure —

D. Cueller

五

CHAPTER 1

It was painful for each of them. For Aiko, it was her memory of losing her father and not having any recollection of her mother. For Oksana, she felt the anguish of becoming a young woman without having her mother there to see her become the warrior that Aiko saw in her. The warrior she would need to become.

The way Aiko was training Oksana wasn't so subtle. The furniture in the living room that Kyle had picked up from around the Portland neighborhood on weekends had been pushed aside forming a makeshift dojo. Aiko had added her own style and flair to Kyle's home with decorations; beautiful subtle hints of reminders of where she grew up in Japan.

Oksana, now fifteen, was every bit the encouraging student who wanted to be a warrior like her mentor, Aiko. Each of them held a bokuto, a Japanese wooden sword about the size of a katana used for training. Aiko lunged and Oksana countered. Oksana could feel her hands getting tired from gripping the handle firmly. A sharp sting to Oksana's hands as the vibrations passed down through the wooden sword as Aiko didn't hold back the crisp, precise, attacking blows.

Aiko could see her young apprentice was getting tired. "Very good, Oksana. You have taken to your training well."

"When do I get to use a real sword?"

Aiko understood Oksana's rush to achieve but knew the discipline and skill she was trying to teach could not be learned overnight. For Aiko, it was a lifetime. It was all she ever knew. The way of a geisha warrior.

"It has only been six months. Why do you need to use a katana?"

"To defend myself. They killed my mother."

"So, you are looking for revenge?"

Oksana knew that was wrong but she needed a way to channel her emotions

Aiko sensed her confusion, "What about looking for the truth instead?"

"Do you know what happened to my mother? How she died?"

"Yes. Kyle and I have discussed it but not in much detail. I know it weighs heavily on Kyle that he could not be there in time to help save your mother's life and his brother Steven's, too."

"I'll bet Kyle wants revenge," Oksana knew her comment came out wrong. "I mean, wouldn't anyone want revenge. What else is it called?"

Aiko knew Oksana was very impressionable at her age and in this state of mind, "How about we don't call it anything and concentrate on the truth and you having a second chance to make a better life for yourself through discipline and training."

"Truth? The truth is my mother is dead and I don't have a chance to be with her ever again. What kind of life is that?"

"Truth comes in many forms. It is not necessarily from words but from our actions."

Oksana has had this conversation before, not exactly, but one like it. She knew a lesson was coming on.

Aiko continued, "If you want to take another life out of revenge, do you not give the power to someone else to take someone you love away from you?"

"If I had the chance to make these men who killed my mother pay, I would."

"So how should I feel about you?"

Oksana thought about it for a moment then realized she had killed Aiko's father. Wouldn't that give Aiko the right to avenge her father? But instead, she was caring for her as a mother, sensei, and mostly…a friend, "I'm sorry, Aiko. You are right."

"So, do you still feel like you are ready to take another man's life?"

Before Oksana had to come up with a deep and reflective response there was a knock at the door.

Oksana put her bokuto on the edge of the table and rushed to the door, "Aiko, Kyle is back!"

Aiko followed Oksana toward the front door as she too was glad to see that Kyle was home.

That thought touched Aiko deeply as she had never felt that way before and never knew if she would ever find such a place in her heart.

What she hid behind her smile was, she was afraid to let Kyle know it was he who made her feel this way.

Aiko was unaware of the dark silhouette of a man moving through the backyard under the cover of darkness. He passed just outside her living room window and took a hiding place in the shadows.

Oksana was just a few feet away from the door when it suddenly burst open. Splinters from the door jamb were fragmented into the air as Oksana's feet felt like they were cast in stone and she was unable to move them out of fear. A large Asian man stood in the doorway dressed all in black. He was armed with a silenced 22 at the ready.

Aiko calmly put her hand on Oksana's shoulder and led her backwards. Oksana followed but her focus stayed on the gun that was pointed right at her.

Aiko could sense Oksana was controlling her breathing to not only slow down her breathing but also her heartbeat. She was using the training Aiko had given her to gain control of the adrenaline that could course through one's body in a time of panic or fear so she could soundly assess her best options.

The large Asian intruder entered the house. His shoulders were almost as wide as the door itself, and he kept a slow steady pace and distance to Aiko as everyone made their way back into the living room area.

The man with the gun, with a slight flick of the wrist, jerked the tip of the silencer side to side to motion his two hostages to go to the center of the room. Aiko noticed the partial tattoo that was half exposed from under the end of his jacket sleeve ended at his wrist, in which he held the gun.

Oksana had noticed that Aiko stopped suddenly. Oksana felt a draft and slowly turned around. She saw that there was a second man, with a slight build had entered through the back-patio doors standing directly behind Aiko and had a gun in the small of her back.

The tension grew more ominous as a third man entered through the front door, using an elaborately carved cane as support of his awkward gait, hobbled into view, "Where is, The Guardian?"

"It is not here," Aiko replied.

Aiko was pistol whipped between the neck and the shoulder blades. The instant pain buckled her knees and she dropped to the floor.

As she went down, she pulled Oksana down with her and they were sitting on the floor eye to eye. Oksana could see the fire in Aiko's eyes.

Aiko's words come back to her, "You have to know when to fight and when to show weakness to give yourself time to survive."

The first man through the door had moved in behind Oksana. He put his 22 back into its shoulder harness. He then reached down, grabbed onto Oksana's ponytail, and pulled her up to her feet by her hair.

"Let's try this again. My name is Isamu-san. You can call me, Mr. Amachi. My associates and I are here for the Guardian. Where is it?"

Amachi gestured with his cane to Onishi who was behind Aiko. Onishi pressed his firm hand down on Aiko's shoulder so she could not get up and proceeded to step onto her fingers, pinning them to the floor. Aiko and Oksana looked at each other and Oksana could see the fear in Aiko's eyes that she had for Oksana if they did not cooperate.

The man grinded his heel hard into the back of Aiko's hand causing a couple of her knuckles to pop.

"I know where it is." Oksana's words felt like a betrayal.

"Don't Oksana. They will kill you."

Aiko's outburst was not taken lightly. The man that was stepping on her hand raised his knee sharply and kicked Aiko in the side of the forehead stunning her, rendering her senseless, and Aiko fell to the floor like a rag doll.

Amachi didn't want to ask again, "If you don't show us, I will kill you for sure."

Oksana, with a slight turn of her head guided the large man who was still holding her by her ponytail, closer to the table next to the dining room window. There was a large scarf covering the sword and the stand itself.

Oksana pulled off the scarf and revealed the Guardian resting on the top support of the display stand.

"And the legend," requested Amachi.

Tagawa, with a slight jerk back on her ponytail, expressed his demands in broken English, "Open it."

Oksana slowly reached out and began to turn the two knobs reversing the yin and yang symbols that made up the design on the front of the wooden knobs. The lower hidden drawer opened.

In the bottom of the drawer was a piece of dry leathery skin about the size of a dollar bill with faded tattoo markings on it.

Oksana reached in and removed it.

Tagawa was so close to Oksana she could feel his breath on the back of her neck as he spoke, "Show it to me."

Oksana raised her hand showing the intruders what they were after. Tagawa reached out with his free hand, took the object and tossed it back to Amachi. Amachi took a good look at it to make sure it was genuine, and it appeared to be so. He took out his cell phone and hit the number at the top of the speed dial.

The room was quiet enough everyone could hear the phone on the other end ringing and eventually the call went through. There was no voice on the other end.

Amachi, very self-assured, "We have the legend." He hung up the phone and slipped it in his inner jacket pocket. He then proceeded to reach into the outer pocket and pulled out what looked like an evidence bag. He took another good look at what he called, The Legend, then slipped it inside the pouch and sealed it. His phone rang once more.

He took the call that had a sense of urgency to it and he started toward the front door. Without turning back, he gave out one last order before he walked out the door, "Kill them both and when you are done, bring me the katana."

Oksana was still within reach of the katana and snatched it quickly from the display stand.

With her left hand holding onto the sword's scabbard and her right on the handle, she used her right thumb to release the sword from its scabbard.

Oksana knew the man behind her would take this as more than just a threat as Aiko had taught her, "You never remove the blade unless you are going to use it."

Tagawa was still able to control her by her ponytail with his left hand and jerked her head back violently, throwing her off balance. Her momentum caused her to throw her arms back above her head.

He reached into the left side of his jacket with his right hand and removed a tanto from its scabbard that was attached to the inner lining of the jacket.

As he removed the small sword he brought it up swiftly, cutting away her ponytail. Freed, Oksana turned around and Tagawa showed he had eight inches of her hair in one hand and the razor sharp tanto in the other.

Oksana showed Tagawa she was still holding onto the Guardian. Oksana slowly removed the Guardian's blade from its scabbard. She could feel her heartbeat increasing and pounding harder in her chest as each inch of the sword was exposed.

As much as she had wanted this moment, Aiko's words came back to her about being ready to take another man's life. Oksana had to make a choice, to show the skills Aiko had given her or play it ineptly. Once the tip of the blade cleared the scabbard, she set the katana on the nearby table, and took a pose with the scabbard.

Both men laughed.

At the sight of Oksana taking a strong stance with the scabbard, the other man, Onishi, finally had something to say, "She doesn't even know which part of the sword to fight with."

Before they could finish they're chuckle, Oksana took a step forward and with a full-on strike, cracked Tagawa, the man who took her ponytail, across the forehead. He was instantly stunned from the blow, dropped the tanto at the feet of Onishi, and brought both of his hands up to his aching head. Oksana took advantage of his open torso and shoved the end of the scabbard into his abdomen just below his rib cage, knocking the wind out of him.

Out of reflex, Tagawa dropped his hands, and that was when Oksana spun around using the full force of her momentum, and struck Tagawa across his throat crushing his larynx. Tagawa grabbed his throat with both hands as he bent over gasping for air. As his head was coming down, Oksana had gripped onto both ends of the scabbard and drove it upward across Tagawa's face, breaking his nose.

A large welt started to form on Tagawa's forehead in the shape of a dragon from the carved insignia on the side of the scabbard as blood violently erupted from his nose. Onishi watched as he saw Tagawa fight to stay alive but within thirty seconds, he was dead.

Onishi reached down and picked up the tanto from the floor, "Okay, let us see what else your sensei has taught you."

Oksana flicked the end of the scabbard toward her opponent who quickly countered and, with the end of the tanto, knocked the scabbard to the side. Oksana had a good two-handed grip on the other end of the scabbard and was able to hold on tightly.

Then it was his turn. With a flick of his wrist he sent the razor-sharp end of the sword slicing toward the center of Oksana's chest. Oksana countered, whirled, and with a surprising move, dropped the hard edge of the scabbard across the back of his hand causing him to release the tanto.

As the sword hung in the air momentarily, Oksana swiped at it, and hit the back of the blade just right, reversing its direction back toward her opponent.
The sword's razor-sharp edge sliced across his forearm. A stream of blood gushed from his arm onto the floor.

Onishi tried to make a quick move to pick up the tanto but Oksana once again countered, which caused him to jump back to avoid being struck by the scabbard. All he had within reach was one of the bokutos. He snatched it from the table, "No more games."

Onishi took a defensive stance with the bokuto. Oksana knew he had the advantage now and she had to get it back. She jabbed at her opponent with the Guardian's scabbard. He countered and struck Oksana across her back, sending her momentum into the table. There in front of her was the Guardian. She picked up the sword. The blade had never felt heavier. This time she felt the weight of her actions as well. She turned and revealed that she now had the scabbard in her left hand and the katana in her dominant right hand. For a split-second Oksana thought she had regained the advantage. Before she could enjoy the moment, her opponent had lashed out and struck the blade of the katana so hard with the bokuto it cut off the end of the wooden training sword and the reverberation sent a jolt of pain into her right hand. Before she could regrip, another blow from her opponent, down the side of the blade, had caught the hilt just above her hand knocking the sword from her grasp.

As the katana skimmed across the floor, the edge of the sword's rounded hilt rolled through the small concentration of Onishi's blood that had pooled on the floor. As the katana's hilt rolled through the blood, its edge left a thin, red trail of a partial sentence of Asian text.

Onishi recognized the pattern in the chain of text which momentarily caught him off guard, which caused him to hesitate. In that moment, the edge of the scabbard Oksana was holding caught her opponent on the side of the neck.

Onishi felt a burst of pain pass through him from head to toe and before he could react, he felt another sharp blow as Oksana cracked him across his shin sending blinding pain back up through his body. This was followed by a blow across his back, sending him down and out for the count.

Oksana looked down at the two men who were lying on the floor. Then she heard Aiko's voice, "You are learning."

Oksana looked back just as Aiko had made it to her feet and was holding the Guardian.

"Who are they?" Oksana asked.

"I believe they are yakuza."

The sound of Kyle's voice startled them as he entered cautiously through the front door with his 9mm Glock drawn, "Hello?" Followed by a very concerned, "What happened to the front door?"

Kyle made his way into the living room and saw the devastation.

As a Portland detective, he had seen crime scenes before but this one was in his own home. This one took on a whole new meaning, especially after he and Aiko had recused Oksana.

He thought they were clear to start a new life together.

"What happened here?"

"Yakuza," Oksana replied with a shrug and a newfound confidence not really comprehending the term.

Kyle saw the drawer to the sword stand was open, "What were these two after?"

"There were three of them," Aiko replied.

Kyle got sense from Aiko the house was secure and holstered his gun, "What happened to the third man?"

"He got away and he took it with him."

"Took what?"

"The legend."

CHAPTER 2

In the Sea of Japan an iceberg about 100 yards in diameter was drifting within a mile of the Northern coast of Japan. The fifty tons of freshwater ice had broken away from a glacier off the Southeastern coast of Russia, in the Sea of Okhotsk. Set adrift, it made its way south in the cold waters of the Oyashio currents that took it through the La Perouse Strait, which was located between the islands of Sakhalin and Hokkaido just North of Japan. A nearby marine research vessel, known as the RAISA, was monitoring its progress.

Aboard the forty-two foot research vessel, thirty-five scientists and crew members were marveling at the wedge-shaped iceberg.

Dr. Akihito was talking to his assistant, "Let the team know it looks like the iceberg's drift is going to pass the island without any unforeseen problems."

"Hai," the assistant replied in the affirmative.

As the assistant walked away, Dr. Akihito's wife joined him on the deck.

"I don't know why you drag me out on these excursions of yours when nothing exciting ever happens. Why can't you start exploring the life we have always talked about?"

"Nothing? Raisa, no one has seen an iceberg this size in the Sea of Japan in hundreds of years. This is history in the making. Besides, I named this vessel after you and this is the first time in a long time you have come out to sea on such a momentous occasion."

"You call seeing an iceberg momentous?"

"Yes. One this close I do, and I wouldn't want to share this moment with anyone else."

"Except with all the other scientists on the ship. How romantic."

"Our investors pay for all of this and what's a little company to keep them happy?"
Raisa shrugged her shoulders, "What happens when it melts? Where's your history?"

"In the data. Raisa, look at this." Dr. Akihito opened his notebook to a map, "An earthquake here in Japan last month sent shockwaves as far as the Bering Sea. It broke off a block of ice the size of Manhattan that caught currents that run south toward Japan. Along the way, it's been slowly melting and during the storm we had two weeks ago, the currents have guided what was left of the iceberg through the La Perouse Straight and on down into the Sea of Japan. This is all very exciting!"

Dr. Akihito guided Raisa closer to the railing and situated her so her back was to the iceberg.

"We are going to make you, my lovely wife, a part of history."

Dr. Akihito took out his iPhone and snapped a few pictures.

Raisa was still not impressed.

"Okay, now for some video," he continued.
As Dr. Akihito started to record, a massive chunk of ice fell away on one side of the iceberg.

The iceberg had drifted into an underwater shelf about fifty feet down. The impact sheared off part of the floating monolith. As the iceberg became unbalanced it started to list to one side. The torque within the iceberg was too much and part of one side of it pulled away. It was a thunderous sound like that of a tree splitting from a lightning strike. Something the crew of the RAISA had never expected to see was now happening. The iceberg began to slowly flip over like a giant humpback whale breaching.

As it rolled, what was once the underside was now a tower of deep blue ice rising out of the sea. It soon began to settle but not for long. Another large piece broke off, sending a large wave toward the RAISA. Everyone on board seemed to have seen the extraordinary event except Raisa. Raisa had heard the splash and saw the excitement on her husband's face as his eyes came up from the monitor on the phone and gazed over her shoulder. Just as she turned around, the entire group was standing in awe as they witnessed the phenomenon.

Everyone began to scramble as they saw a set of fifteen-foot waves heading their direction.
The Captain of the vessel began to shout out orders.

"Right full rudder, now! Let's get the ship's bow turned into the direction of that first wave and take them head-on."

The large vessel came about just as the first wave cut across its bow. The ship sliced through the wave like butter as the bow rose and fell with not much mercy.

The crew and passengers of the research vessel, RAISA, road out the waves like a kiddy ride at Disneyland.

Dr. Akihito held onto his wife and the guardrail together to help keep her steady as the ship took on one wave after another with ease.

The small turbulence caused him to lose his grip on his iPhone and he dropped it overboard.

The phone sank and drifted down to a shallow coral reef fifty feet below. As it hit the bottom, there was a light, muffled bong sound as it hit something metal. The phone settled into the murky water it stirred up a sleeping eel that slithered away. As it did, its tail wiped away the sediment from the side of the cast iron object. There on the side of a ship's bell was the name, AMADA.

Raisa stood still huddled in her husband's arms as the ship came to rest once again on the calming sea. Raisa gained her composure and looked at her husband.

"Are you okay, Raisa?" her husband asked.

"Yes. This is why I don't like to be out here. You know I don't like the large waves and the rocking motion of the ship."

"Not to worry, my dear, it's over now."

The Captain joined them on deck, "Excuse me, Doctor."

"Yes, what is it?"

"We've picked something up on radar. There appears to be a large mass of some kind that is located on the shelf right below us. From the looks of it, it appeared to be man-made and very old."

Dr. Akihito kissed his wife, "Is history exciting enough for you now?"

CHAPTER 3

Standing outside his house, Kyle was worried that one day the past they thought they left behind would return, and it had. Kyle had to refocus to catch up to what police detective, James DeMint, was asking him.

"How is the girl doing, Kyle?"

"Oksana is doing pretty good considering three men all dressed in black just broke into her home and tried to kill her and Aiko. How do you think she should be doing?"

"Do you know what these guys were after? Is there anything missing?"

"No, not really. I got here after it was all over. Aiko said Oksana went to answer the door thinking it was me, as soon as she turned the door handle, two men barged their way in and Aiko was able to subdue the both of them."

Kyle noticed Aiko as she walked out onto the front porch with Oksana who was still a little shaken. Now that he saw them together, DeMint realized just how much they meant to Kyle, and he couldn't take his eyes off of them.

Det. DeMint noticed the worry on Aiko's face as she held onto Oksana.

A rookie officer by the name of Hamilton approached DeMint and caught him off guard with his question, "Why the black out? What's makes this case so special?"

DeMint turned his attention to the young officer and tilted his head down to look over the top rim of his classes, "I know you're new to Portland so I'll let that one slide. One, don't ever question my reasons for keeping this one out of the media. Two, did you do any of your homework on the city you were coming to work in? If you had read up on the police reports like you were asked to, you would have read about a case that took place about six months ago involving Det. Kyle Morrell."

"That is Kyle Morrell?" The young officer had done his homework but had only skimmed over the case file, but he did understand enough of it to know it was a big case. "He was the one who took down the human trafficking ring and killed all of the Masato family."

"Not quite. That woman he is with on the porch is Aiko Masato."

"I heard she was a concubine."

DeMint grabbed the shoulder of the young officer firmly, "I don't want to ever hear those words come out of your mouth again. If you want to know who she is, go inside the house and you will see."

DeMint walked the officer over to the entrance and gestured him to go take a look at the crime scene inside the house. Once the officer slipped past Kyle and entered the house, DeMint got a good look at Oksana and saw she was shaken but going to be okay.

DeMint got up close to Kyle and with deep concern asked, "Is there someplace you can go until we get these guys ID'd and make sure the house is safe before you return?"

Aiko could hear what the officer was asking and gave Kyle a nod letting him know she and Oksana were okay. The look on Kyle's face was more than just concern. He couldn't help but show the love he felt for Aiko.

DeMint knew they needed their space and rejoined his team near the street to make sure the perimeter was secure.

Kyle gave Aiko and Oksana a hug and then led them back to the house.

As they went in, Officer Hamilton came out of the house a little paler than when he went in, and promptly found a bush to relieve himself of his lunch as the crime scene was a lot more than he expected.

A little while later, Aiko and Oksana joined Kyle in the entryway with their bags packed. He had just finished checking his iPhone and turned it off.

"We need to get off the grid for a while. Once we get in the car we need to remove the batteries from our cell phones until we need them."

Oksana knew they may not be coming back for a while, "Where are we going?"

Kyle wanted to keep the conversation light, "Where do you want to go?"

Oksana gave an enthusiastic, "The beach!"

"Okay, the beach it is." Kyle grabbed the bags, "Do we have everything?"

Aiko walked over to the display stand and removed the katana, known as The Guardian. Now she was ready.

Outside in the front yard, Det. DeMint, was talking to a patrol officer who was telling him they found a car they thought might belong to the two men involved in the home invasion. One of which was now in custody, handcuffed to a gurney, in the back of an ambulance.

As Kyle, Aiko, and Oksana walked by DeMint, he got Kyle's attention, "Where are you headed? We may need to contact you if we have any more questions about what happened here tonight."

Oksana paused when she heard Kyle's reply, "I think we'll head up to the mountains for a few days. I have a friend who has a cabin up near Mount Hood."

Aiko put her arm around Oksana's shoulder and kept her moving towards Kyle's car. After Kyle finished talking to DeMint, he began to head in the direction of his car to join Aiko and Oksana for a well needed road trip.

DeMint's comment didn't seem to matter that much to Kyle, "As soon as we have something, I'll give you call."

DeMint took a look around and saw the crowd taking pictures on their cell phones, encroaching too much of the scene. He asked one of his men to make sure the neighbors stay behind the crime scene tape. The officer asked the crowd to step back.

He noticed a middle-aged Asian man with a cane turn and walk away before he could get a good look at him.

Once the Asian man was a good distance away he looked back over his shoulder at the crime scene. It was Amachi.

Kyle adjusted the rearview mirror so he could take one last look at the house. As the distance grew, he also hoped to put a distance on the pain he was causing Aiko and Oksana, having to uproot them once again trying to stay ahead of the danger. He felt the energy start to drain from him with each breath as he thought about if he could keep them safe. He may not have all the answers but he did know one thing, if to came down to it, he would give his life to save theirs.

Kyle collected his thoughts, "We may not be able to come back here if what you said was true. Aiko, you really think those guys were yakuza?"

"Yes, I think so. I saw a few of their tattoos. They have a very distinct style."

"Kyle?"

"Yes, Oksana."

"I heard you tell that officer we were heading to Mount Hood." Oksana needed some clarification, "I thought we were going to the beach?"

"We are. I just needed to make sure we were going to have some family time to ourselves."

"Kyle."

"Yes, Oksana."

"Are we still in danger?"

Aiko could sense a little bit fear of the unknown in Oksana, "Oksana, when you are with Kyle and myself, I do not want you to be afraid. We will always be looking out for you."

Oksana was quiet. Kyle could see Oksana in the rearview mirror starting to cry.

"What is it, Oksana?" Kyle asked.

Oksana thought about her words before asking,

"Can you tell me why Victor wanted to sell me?"

Kyle had to think about how much he wanted to expose Oksana to the world of human trafficking, "Once Victor found out he was not your father, your mother wanted to take you away, and that made him very angry. He wanted to punish your mom so I guess he thought if he couldn't have you, he didn't want your mom to have you either."

"So, he wanted to sell me?"

"That is why my brother Steven was sent to help you."

"Why was my price the highest on the list?"

Kyle had to rethink his strategy but before he could answer, Aiko replied, "Because, Oksana, you are very special and with such a high price maybe your father really didn't think anyone could afford you and he would have to keep you."

"But someone did buy me and before my mom could kill him, the man removed my clothes and…"

Kyle pulled the car over onto the side of the road. He was angry and hurt for Oksana.

He turned around as best he could and pulled Oksana close to him, "I'm sorry. I didn't know."

"The same thing happened to me, Oksana," Aiko revealed. "I was not sold but I was about the same age as you. The first man I was with was not my choice. You know I was raised in an orphanage and I was told I had been adopted but I was left there to be trained. One of my classes was in how to be with a man."

Kyle's heart couldn't sink any further and he didn't want to know, but this might be the only time it would be said so he let Aiko continue.

"As it turned out, that man waited until I was a young woman before he brought me home. I performed as I was taught until the day I found out he was my father.

****

The day had been warm so as they arrived at the coast, the cool night air had drawn in a thick blanket of fog off the ocean. As Kyle drove up to the beach house it was dark. The headlights from the car only added to the mystery that lay ahead as Kyle asked Aiko to stay behind with Oksana while he checked out the old blue grey coastal hideaway.

Kyle followed the cobblestone path that led to the house and as he got closer he could make out the white door frame which at least gave him a direction to the front porch.

He used the hide-a-way key that he found under the wooden decorative figure of a seagull that sat on the edge of the porch. Once inside he took a good look around.

When he felt everything was in order, he turned on the gas fireplace, then went to help Aiko and Oksana bring in the bags.

Once they were settled in, Oksana was in the guest room unpacking, and making sure no nasty things were lurking under the bed.

In the living room, Aiko had found a blanket and had covered her and Kyle's legs as they nestled into each other on the couch.

"Thank you, Kyle, for keeping your promise. Oksana really wanted to come here."

"Of course. She's been through a lot and you have been great with her. She seems to be able to handle herself with the sword."

"She did not use the katana. Her opponent had it until she disarmed him."

"She did all that with one of those stick things?"

"No, she used the sword's scabbard. She is not ready to use the katana. It takes more than a few lessons. It takes years of discipline before she can to take on that responsibility."

"She sure made a case for being a fast learner."

"She was lucky. They did not respect her but next time they will not make that same mistake."

Oksana had been listening from the doorway of her room, "But I am ready." Oksana made her way over and took a seat at the end of the couch.

Aiko respectfully disagreed, "No, you are not." Oksana was sticking to her guns, "But I saved your life."

"You were only able to do what you did because they saw you as a girl, not a student."

"So you will continue to teach me?"

Kyle felt he had to stand up for what Oksana was able to do today, "I'm sure Aiko will be happy to teach you. Someday you too can be as good as Aiko."

Aiko gave Kyle a look that caused him to almost flinch as if she had just smacked him one, "Oksana, why don't you finish unpacking and then we will see what we can find to make something for dinner."

That brought a smile to her face as she headed off to her room because next to katana training, she really liked it when Aiko taught her to cook Asian style food. Especially when they used the wok and chop sticks. Oksana loved to watch Kyle try to use them and drop his food. Then she would reach over and pick it up with her chop sticks and feed him. It would even bring a smile to Aiko's face.

Right now, Aiko's face was saying something else, "Kyle…"

Aiko, we don't know what's going to happen over the next few days but let's just get through tonight without feeling like it is going to be our last."

"Kyle…"

"Hey, you two are closer than you think. She too has lost her mother and from what I can see, you both are good for each other." Kyle felt himself getting lost in Aiko's eyes, "You've changed my life as well." The kiss he gave her was soft and tender. She too understood and felt his meaning like it was her own.

"I am not worthy of your love, Kyle. I am..."

"You're perfect."

"No, I am not. I am afraid my past has caught up with me once again and now it has put you both in danger."

"I'm all in, Aiko."

Oksana had to let her feelings be known, "So am I." Once again Oksana joined them on the couch and gave Kyle a hug, "We are family now."

Aiko was trying to understand this little girl who was growing up right in front of her, "But you have a father."

"A father who doesn't even know I exist."

CHAPTER 4

Outside Walter Reed Hospital three black cars were parked near the entrance. Each of the two cars at either end were used for the Secret Service agents who were standing alongside, keeping anyone who showed interest at bay. The heavy duty built up Cadillac, known as The Beast, was in between. One of the agents raised his hand to his earpiece then replied through the mic hidden in his cuff.

Inside the hallway of the Intensive Care Unit one of the Secret Service agents acknowledged his colleagues. He turned toward the agent that was on guard in front of the door to an exam room and told him that everything was clear. Then with a hand gesture he let the men at each end of the hallway know the same.

Dr. Riggs had his iPad at the ready and was going over a few notes from the results of a series of tests as he approached the door to the guarded exam room.

One of the Agents opened the door for the doctor and followed him in.

As Dr. Riggs entered, his patient had lost his patience, "I hope this isn't going to take much longer. You know I have a country to run. I just got an urgent call and I'll be needing to head back to the White House. Can you please send the results over at your earliest convenience?"

"Well, right now you're not POTUS you're my patient. The country is just going to have to wait its turn. We have a preliminary result of your test that I need to go over with you."

"What is it?"

Dr. Riggs looked at the Agent on duty then back at the President, "Can we have the room?"

President Dalton motioned to his men to leave, "Give us the room."

The two Secret Service agents headed to the door. One took a position just down the hall as the other stood just outside the door.

Once the door was closed, Dr. Riggs scrolled down to the next page on Dalton's chart and still had to take a moment to organize his thoughts.

Dalton saw the anguish in his doctor's face, "What is it?"

"Leukemia."

Dalton had to take in the possibility of not only losing his Presidency but his life, "Are you sure about this? Could it be something else?"

The Doctor didn't have to look at his chart again, he knew the results weren't going to change, "You came in complaining of feeling you might be coming down with the flu, having lost some weight recently, and having night sweats."

"Could it just be signs of stress that comes with the job."

"Sure, but these are also signs that we look for when making this kind of diagnosis. Your test results came back with high numbers of abnormal white blood cells. I didn't see it anywhere in your family history. We need to be sure, therefore I want to run your labs again but all indications are telling us that it's leukemia."

"If it is, did we catch it in time? Is there a treatment that can lead us to a cure?"

"We caught it early but how it progresses varies from patient to patient. I need to run a full series of tests to make sure where we are with this. If it turns out you do have it, one of the treatments is to do a bone marrow transplant, as long as we can find a donor match. Usually the best results come from an immediate family member."

Dalton got a very concerned look on his face. He already knew his children had the same blood type as their mother which was different than his own. As he was completing his thought, he could feel his shoulders slumping as each breath he drew became heavier as did his chances for survival were taxing his mind. With another deep breath, he sensed his vision of the future for life, love, and country were dissipating as well.

Dr. Riggs scrolled deeper into Dalton's chart, "Don't you have a sister in Alabama?"

"My sister passed away a few years ago, in a car accident, other than that, I don't have any other siblings."

"What about your son or daughter? They could be a match. If they are, we can then do what is called an Allogenic bone marrow transplant. We'll take stem cells from the donor and see if they are a good match for you."

"What if they're not a match?"

"Then we'll have to check the national bone marrow registry, and with your blood type being B positive, that is a narrow window to work with."

"How narrow?"

Before Dr. Riggs could answer, a Secret Service agent knocked and opened the door. The agent walked over to the president, leaned in, and whispered something in Dalton's ear.

Before the agent could finish his sentence, Dalton interrupted, "What are you talking about?"

CHAPTER 5

The beach house was located on a quiet strip of land with a backyard view to die for, the Oregon coast. The house belonged to a longtime friend of Kyle's who used it as an Airbnb but happened to be available and Kyle took advantage of his friend's offer to get lost for a while. For the moment, as long as they were all together, this was home. At the same time, he knew wherever they were they were in danger, and that was not the home he had imagined. Even that was a dream he thought. Like a dream, he only saw pieces at a time but what he saw, he found himself becoming someone else. Once where he only thought of himself he now wanted to share his life with Aiko and Oksana. After all they had been through as individuals, circumstance had brought their worlds together, and together he found a purpose.

From inside the living room, Kyle was looking through the sliding glass doors that led out to the back patio. He watched as Oksana was enjoying the waves crashing onto the shore. She seemed to be in a trance as if she couldn't feel the cool air blowing through her hair. Her eyes fixed on the ocean as one wave rolled in after another. It crossed his mind, was she also dreaming of being here with them or was she just another lost girl wondering what life had given her at such a young age?

Oksana was stirred from her moment of bliss as the seventh wave with its stronger push up the shore quickly surrounded her bare feet causing her to jump back and run toward the higher ground. Kyle saw her wave at him and smile. He smiled and waved back as she took a seat in lawn chair she had borrowed from the back patio. Kyle saw the child in her and the strength of the young woman she was becoming.

One word came to mind as he watched Oksana running back up the beach toward him. Pride.

Kyle reached into his pocket of his grey hoodie and retrieved the small gift box. He opened it, peeked inside, and smiled. He closed the lid, then closed his eyes, and said a small prayer. It was just a small token of how he really felt but he hoped Aiko knew that too.

Aiko tested the water for her bath and finding it at the right temperature, she slipped off her robe and placed it on the wooden chair that sat at the end of the cast iron tub. She turned off the water, stepped into the tub, then lowered herself into the welcoming sensation of stopping time, at least for a little while.

The bathroom's wooden walls and floor beaded the droplets of water from the steam that gave it a spa type atmosphere.

Aiko heard the bathroom door being slowly opened. She looked over and saw Oksana peeking in.

"I have something for you, Aiko."

Oksana entered and walked up with both hands behind her back.

"What do you have there, Oksana?"

"Guess."

"Is it a seashell from the beach?"

"No." Oksana showed Aiko a small pink bottle and a small round candle, "It's time for a bubble bath."

"I have never had a bubble bath."

Before Aiko could say anything more, Oksana had the lid off and was pouring the solution into Aiko's bath water.

"This is going to be so much fun," Oksana said as Aiko just sat there watching Oksana smiling and giggling.

"And it makes your skin so soft."

All Aiko could do was smile as she watched Oksana start to swish her hands in the water making bubbles. Then Aiko began to help her and soon they had a tub filled with flower scented bubbles.

Oksana took a towel and folded it into a small pillow and put it behind Aiko's neck, "Now rest your head back and close your eyes."

Aiko did as she was told. Oksana lit the candle and set it on the edge of the counter closest to the tub.

Aiko took a peek as Oksana left the room and thought that she could get used to having a bubble bath once in a while.

Aiko had only had five minutes to herself before Kyle knocked gently on the door then entered.

She didn't mind as he moved her robe to one side and took a seat on the edge of the chair.

Aiko knew by the way Kyle looked at her he had deeper feelings than she could express for him. It was harder for her. She had always been told how to feel and now as she looked into Kyle's eyes, she could sense he wanted her to feel the same way as he did. There was just one thing, she had been trained in the art of love, not love itself.

Aiko was waiting for Kyle to say something that would help her to understand.

It had crossed her mind that if he couldn't find the words, the conversation would have to wait, and that was okay with Aiko.

"Well look at you…"

"I'm having a bubble bath."

"Yes, you are."

"It is my first one."

"Oksana said she wanted to do something nice for you."

Aiko knew she caught Kyle off guard by his reaction when she said, "Oksana knows."

"Knows what?"

"Who her father is. She was asking me about him the other day."

"And what did you tell her?"

"What she already knew. That he's the President of the United States."

Neither Kyle nor Aiko could top that so the conversation ended there.

Aiko rubbed the bar of soap on the wash cloth then began to wash her shoulders. Kyle stood up, moved the chair to the other end of the tub, took the wash cloth from Aiko, and began to wash her shoulders for her. It took a minute for Aiko to let herself enjoy the tender moment. It wasn't like before in the shower when they had to break into the boathouse and use the shower to get warm. This was allowing someone in to where no one had been before; in her heart. She knew Kyle was just trying to be romantic and could feel it in the way his hands caressed her. He was always gentle with her and never made her feel uncomfortable. That took a bit of getting used to as she was finding that it took less time than before to feel wanted for her heart and soul and not for just her body.

Aiko had closed her eyes and let herself drift off a bit.

Kyle kept his voice low, "You look relaxed."

"I am. I like this tub."

"Maybe I'll get you one for your birthday."

"Why would you do that?"

"Because you look beautiful in it. Then again, that would be a present for me."

Aiko had a very quiet demeanor. She pulled her knees up to her chest, crossed her arms on her knees, then rested her head onto her arms.

Kyle began to wash her hair and Aiko tilted her head back to get her hair wet.

As she did, Kyle leaned in and gave her a light kiss. He continued to wash her hair then she helped him to rinse it. Kyle took the wash cloth and used the suds from the bubble bath to wash her arms and shoulders. Kyle could feel the tension in Aiko starting to relax as she let her legs slip down into the tub. As her legs submerged the bubbles drifted across the water leaving Kyle with a clear view of Aiko's supple breasts. He let his hand with the wash cloth follow the curve of her neck then slip under the water to wash her upper body. He knew what he felt for Aiko was real and hoped Aiko could sense not only the pleasure but his heart. Kyle felt she understood as he could feel her heartbeat pounding like a drum in the palm of his hand.

Kyle kissed Aiko once again but this time with a bit more passion.

Kyle took a breath, "I love you, Aiko." Kyle could feel she was closing herself off again, "What's the matter?"

"You would not understand."

"Try me."

"I was put into an orphanage when I was a very young girl. Records were lost. I do not know my birthday."

Kyle caressed Aiko willing the tension to leave her body. With a little more attention, he got her to open up and rest her head back on the edge of the tub.

He leaned over and gave her a light kiss on the lips. After she opened her eyes, she saw that Kyle was holding a small gift box in front of her, "It happens to be today."

Aiko opened the box. Inside was a necklace that had a

pendent with a yin and yang symbol on it carved out of jade.

Aiko smiled, "I don't understand."

"Oksana has been going through the files on the flash drive and a couple weeks ago, she came across another file that pertained to you. It showed your father had been tracking your every move from the day you were placed into the orphanage, all through your training, and up until you started at Masato Enterprises."

Aiko at first felt ashamed but then she knew Kyle never would hold that against her. He told her a quote she once told him, "Although the journey was hard, it is who we are, and has placed us in each other's path."

Kyle let Aiko in on another little find, "It also had a note about your place of birth and the day you were born. When she showed it to me, we decided to get you a gift. Oksana picked it out."

Kyle helped Aiko remove the necklace from the box and he placed it around her neck. After he set the clasp, he adjusted the pendent so it laid flat on her skin just above her cleavage.

Aiko touched it and could feel her heart beating beneath it, "I have never received such a special gift."

They kissed once more to say what words could not.

Kyle stood. Aiko pulled the plug from the tub, then Kyle helped Aiko to stand and as the water drained, Kyle helped Aiko dry off.

They both enjoyed the sensuality of feeling the soft towel as a thin barrier as they each guided the other's hands to caress over and around the curves of Aiko's body. Another kiss was very warm and welcome as Kyle lifted Aiko from the tub and lowered her onto the floor rug. He knelt and dried her legs. His hands following the contours of her thighs, calves, and then lifted one foot at a time as Kyle dried her feet.

When he was done, he gave a soft kiss next to her belly button. Aiko ran her hands through his hair then tried to guide him up from his knees. She felt a little resistance at first but then Kyle stood and their lips made contact once more. Kyle's eyes had a twinkle in them brighter than the smile on his face.

Aiko could sense the love Kyle was willing to share but was still coming to an understanding within herself trying to redefine her definition of love.

She was not resisting. She was relearning.

Kyle had her robe open and waiting for her. He watched as Aiko stepped into her panties and pulled them up along her thighs. He then slipped her into the comfort of her robe and wrapped his arms around her. The warmth of the bath had relaxed her, but her heart was pounding out of her chest and Kyle could feel it through her robe as they clasped hands between her breasts.

Aiko leaned her head back into Kyle's chest, tilted her head, and they kissed. Kyle could feel Aiko pull open their arms and Kyle released her.

Aiko moved over next to the mirror and Kyle watched her as she opened her robe enough at the top so the pendent could still be seen. Aiko caught Kyle's reflection in the mirror and saw the way he truly looked at her, with all his heart. She felt grateful to have him and Oksana in her life, "Thank you."

"You're welcome."

Kyle tried to kiss Aiko one more time but she slipped past him, "I need to thank Oksana. Like you said, it was she who picked it out."

Kyle could only smile as he watched her walk away from him. He enjoyed that view as well.

Aiko could sense him looking at her and glanced back over her shoulder, "Are you going to just stand there and gawk?"

Kyle nodded then began to follow as he talked to himself, "Believe me. You're worth the gawk."

CHAPTER 6

Kyle joined Aiko in the living room and took a seat on the couch opposite her. Aiko had taken the chair on the far side of the coffee table. In between them on the table was the Guardian. Kyle picked up the one of a kind katana and admired it even more as he learned its history and why so many men had died over it. But that just raised more questions. Why were they willing to kill for it?

Kyle took a closer look at the dried blood that was clinging to the edge of the katana's hilt, "So, this sword is more than just a weapon, it is a piece of art. Did you see the pattern it left on the floor?"

"Yes. It looks to be an ancient form of Japanese text."

"Did you know the writing was there as part of the hilt?"

"No."

Kyle looked over and saw Oksana's backpack. He looked inside and found a pencil and a piece of paper. He rubbed the edge of the pointed lead end of the pencil onto the paper laying down a dusting of the lead shavings.

Kyle then peeled off specs of dried blood from the hilt giving it a clean edge. He rolled the katana's hilt across the micro pieces of lead and then carefully lifted the hilt over to a clean piece of paper and rolled out the hilt like a wheel. There, in its tracks, was a line of Japanese text.

Kyle was anxious, "Can you read it?"

Aiko turned the paper in her direction and with the pencil drew a line where she thought the sentence began and ended, "Some of it. From what I can read, it looks incomplete."

"So, do you think that is why Pankov was after the tanto and the katana? He must already have the middle one and is trying to complete the set.

Aiko never knew about these clues and came to the conclusion that someone was way ahead of them, "Yes, but for who?"

"Maybe the same person who sent the yakuza to the house to retrieve the legend."

"But why take something as important as the legend and risk leaving the katana behind?"

Kyle was now just as confused as Aiko, "That begs the question of who sent them and how did they know about the hidden drawer in the katana's display stand? Who else even knew we had it?"

"The only person who knew we had the Guardian. Pankov."

"These weren't Pankov's men. He must have been working for someone else when he was after the tanto."

Oksana came in from the patio. She noticed someone had moved her backpack and the closer she got to the table, she could see the mysterious writing in graphite on the paper. She joined Kyle on the couch.

Kyle saw her curiosity and asked Oksana a question before she could ask one of her own, "Oksana, what did the man say exactly when he grabbed you?"

"First, he asked, where was the Guardian? Then he told me to open the drawer."

Oksana was still trying to read the hieroglyphics from the paper upside down.

Aiko had to get her to refocus, "Did they say anything else that stood out?"

"No. Not that I can remember. He just tossed the leather thing to the other guy and then that guy made a phone call."

Oksana touched the edge of the katana's hilt and felt the graphite dust on her finger tips and put two and two together, "Cool."

Kyle asked, "Did you hear any other names or who he might be talking to?"

"No, he just said, that he had the legend. Then he told the other two guys to kill us, and then he left."

Kyle still had too many unanswered questions, "Are you sure he wasn't talking about the sword? I thought the legend was the sword."

Aiko was starting to remember small pieces of her past that were now starting to make sense, "The swords are a part of our family history and go back hundreds of years but that is no legend.

"What do you mean?"

"I think the legend refers to a story I first heard when I was a child in the orphanage. My father used to tell me I was named after it."

Kyle felt a shot of adrenaline just start his heart, "So, you know what it means?"

"No."

"Then why were they willing to kill us over a piece of leather?" Oksana asked.

In the time it took Oksana to ask, Aiko may have found the answer. "It's not just a piece of leather, it's a piece of dried skin, and those markings on it are part of a tattoo."

Oksana's mouth went dry, "Gross. Why would anyone want to save that?"

Kyle was homing in on Aiko's logic, "It must be very important to have been hidden all these years."

Aiko had a moment of clarity, "Maybe because it's not just about a legend but is an actual legend. Those markings tell how to read something."

Oksana felt the same rush as Kyle, "Like a map. Maps have legends."

Kyle was intrigued, "You might be onto something, Oksana. Who would put a tattoo of a map on themselves?"

Aiko knew, "The yakuza."

Kyle and Oksana had the same thought but Oksana got it out first, "Really, I was right?"

Aiko continued, "Yes. For centuries, secrets have long been the responsibility of the yakuza warriors. What better place to hide a secret than a piece of art on a warrior who was willing to die to protect its secret?"

Oksana felt the rush, again, "I think I've seen one of those tattoos."

Now Kyle felt he was lagging just a bit behind, "Where?"

Oksana reached down and picked up her backpack. She removed a flash drive from the side pocket and held it out in her palm for Aiko and Kyle.

Kyle was hungry for answers, "Let's see what you've got."

Oksana removed her laptop from her backpack, inserted the flash drive, and went right to a set of folders marked: Pictures.

"This file was a sub-file I pulled off Victor's laptop."

Oksana brought up a picture of a framed image of an elaborate tattoo on an Asian man's back and turned the laptop to show Aiko and Kyle.

Aiko recognized the art. "Yes. That is a typical tattoo that a yakuza would have."

Oksana saw the large Asian man who's back was covered with elaborate tattoos from his shoulder blades, down across his buttocks, and on down to his mid-thigh.

Oksana was confused, "I thought yakuza meant he was like a ninja? Like the guys who attacked us. According to this, these guys are also known as, gokudo, and are members of organized crime. But the Japanese police call them..."

Aiko helped Oksana with the translation, "Boryokudan. It means, violence group."

Kyle was following along and took over, "And the yakuza refer to themselves as, ninko dantai, meaning chivalrous organizations and have over one-hundred thousand members."

Oksana touched the screen and passed her finger across the tattoo, "Is it painful?"

"It can be very painful." Aiko was speaking from experience.

"Does it still hurt?"

"No." Aiko knew Oksana was curious and had seen only glimpses of her tattoo so Aiko turned and lowered the back of her robe down to her waist.

Oksana was in awe at the sight of the black and white tiger stripes that covered Aiko from width of her shoulders down to the small of her back, "Wow."

Oksana couldn't help herself and reached out and touched Aiko between her should blades. Aiko's skin was soft, smooth to the touch.

Kyle remembered the story of when she got the tattoo, not as art, but as notice to all others that she belonged to Ichiro Masato.

He knew the pain it represented but he only ever let Aiko know it was just a part of everything he loved about her.

Kyle reached out and put his hand next to Oksana's then gently slid the palm of his hand down her back, "It's beautiful, isn't Oksana?"

"Yes," and without missing a heartbeat, "Can I get one?"

Kyle and Aiko both had an immediate and resounding reply, "No!"

Aiko closed her robe and Kyle took another look at the yakuza tattoo and felt like he had a clear direction to pursue, "This tattoo is still on a man. The one we are looking for is not. Oksana, do you have any other pictures like this one in that file?"

Oksana slid the curser over and clicked one step back to get back into the file and opened an array of images for Kyle to choose from.

Kyle saw one he liked, "Can you click on that one and make it larger for me?"

The full image showed what is known as a human pelt that has been preserved and framed behind a sheet of non-breakable glass hanging in a museum.

Aiko leaned in to get a better look, "Can you get any information from the photo to tell us anything about its whereabouts?"

Oksana zoomed in on a description card that was on the wall next to the display frame. On the corner of the card was the logo for the museum.

Oksana read it aloud, "The Tokyo Metropolitan Museum."

Aiko could hear the discouragement in Kyle's voice, "A lot of good that does us."

"Actually, it does," Oksana replied as she started a google search.

A couple of lines down on the page was a cross-reference for the George Anthony Studios and she clicked on it.

Oksana continued reading, "It says here that there is an exhibit going on right now, from Tokyo, here in Portland at a local art studio." Oksana scrolled down through the images and came across pictures of human Japanese yakuza pelts.

Aiko looked at Kyle who came up with the same reasoning, "That's why they need the legend. Whatever it is, it's happening now."

Kyle made one more request of Oksana, "Can you get us an address of that studio?"

Oksana was one step ahead of Kyle and showed him the screen where she had already brought up an image of the George Anthony Studios, the corresponding address, a map with directions, and the hours the studio was open to the public.

CHAPTER 7

The exterior of the George Anthony Studios was made up of three large brick façades. The center façade had a series of about 10 steps that led up to the three main doors. Each door had an extended frame to allow more natural light into the lobby of the Museum.

A brand-new white BMW with tinted windows pulled up in front of the entrance.

A beautiful Asian business woman in her early 30's, impeccably dressed, exited the car from the back-passenger seat followed by her 16-year-old son. As they both ascended the stairs, a man who seemed to be expecting their arrival, opened the center door allowing them not to hesitate as they entered the building. Once inside, the man motioned to the driver of the BMW who then drove off to park and be on standby.

The interior of the lobby had a warm, welcome feeling about it as the light passed through the windows not only heating the room, but seemed to bounce off almost every surface, giving the room a glow. In the back center of the room was a large bronze statue of a Japanese warrior on horseback.

The Asian woman flashed her credentials as they walked past the reception area, through the lobby, and into the Museum.

Once inside of the exhibit area she took a moment to look around, not at the artwork, but for the man who was hosting her exhibit, George Anthony. It didn't take long before she recognized her host from his photographs. Once they made eye contact it only took a few steps before they were introducing themselves to one another with a bow. One thing George noticed as they exchanged business cards was that the woman had a scar running down the top of her thumb.

"Hello Mr. Anthony. My name is Sakura Konishi and this is my son, Zen. It is nice to finally meet you."

"I'm sorry it has taken so long to finally meet you, Ms. Konishi." George extended his hand and greeted Zen with a firm handshake, "You can call me Tony if you like." George returned his focus back to Sakura, "It looks like the exhibit is going very well. We are all ready for tonight's reception."

"I'm sure everything will be in order and that there will be no surprises."

In a nearby adjoining room, Kyle, Aiko, and Oksana were looking at the displays of human pelts that were meticulously framed.

The fused exterior light through the room's domed skylight along with the boldness of the deep red walls, accented the dark wood of the frame and drew the observer's eye to focus on the brilliant colors that made up the exquisite tattoos.

There were wooden benches in the middle of the room but none of the patrons were using them. Everyone seemed to be standing as close as they could to get the best view of the details in each of the pieces of art.

Oksana could not get any closer without falling over the red velvet rope that was used as a soft barrier to keep guests from touching the glass of the display.

Oksana pointed to one of the human pelts, "Look here, Aiko. This one has a piece missing."

"Yes. You are right, Oksana, but let's not get too close."

Oksana took out her iPhone and took a few pictures of the human pelts along with other pieces of art that were on display.

Kyle not only noticed the craftsmanship in the tattoos but also the skill it must have taken to remove the human pelts, "I can't believe someone actually took the time to remove these from someone just so they could be on display."

"It is about honor," Aiko interjected. "These men were great warriors and their service will live on in this art."

Oksana could still not believe what she was seeing, "Are these for real?"

Oksana got an answer from a voice she did not recognize.

"Yes. They are for real," Zen replied.

Oksana turned to see a Japanese boy, a little taller than her, and about a couple of years older.

She then refocused on the human pelt.

Zen saw his opportunity to try and freak Oksana out with his knowledge of the display, "Did you know in order to get the best quality of the skin they have to remove it with a scalpel as soon as possible so it doesn't start to decompose?"

Oksana wasn't going to let him get to her, "Really?"

"Yes." Zen wasn't giving up, "There are two ways to preserve the tissue. One is called, the wet method, where they keep the skin in jars filled with glycerin or a type of formaldehyde."

Oksana was right on it, "And what is the other method?"

Now Zen had to dig in and try a little harder to get to Oksana, "Well, after they scrape on the reverse side of the skin removing it from the muscles underneath, it is then stretched and pinned out to dry so it doesn't have a chance to shrink."

Oksana only had one answer, "Cool."

Zen had another card to play, "Did you see the severed finger?"

Oksana let Zen show her the next display case. The card at the edge of the case read: Yubitzume.

Oksana had to ask, "What does that mean?"

"It's when a yakuza has to cut off his little finger and give it to his boss as a form of penance or apology."

"What good does that do?"

"When one uses a samurai sword, you use the bottom three fingers of each hand to grip the katana firmly. If you have lost a finger?"

"I guess then that could be a problem," Oksana replied, then walked over to the next glassed-in display that had a card that read: The Ako Incident, 1700.

The display had an old tanto on a wooden stand.

Oksana recognized the small eleven inch dagger, "That's a tanto. What does Ako mean?"

"That refers the story of the forty-seven Ronin."

"What happened to them?"

"When I was younger, I remember my uncle telling me the story about the revenge of the forty-seven Ronin. A couple of hundred years ago, there were these forty-seven samurai warriors who had a vendetta out for the death of their master. One day their lord, Asano Naganori, was compelled to commit seppuku for assaulting a court official."

Oksana tilted her head like a confused puppy.
Zen motioned across his belly with both hands, "You know, harikari."

"Oh, yeah," Oksana replied.

"These men were now, Ronin. They had no master. So, then they waited a whole year to get revenge by killing that same official who was named, Yoshinaka.
Now, the same honor they held for their master compelled them to also commit harikari for committing his murder."

Zen made the same two-handed motion across his belly, "All forty-seven of them."

Aiko and Kyle walked up behind Oksana just as Sakura stepped in next to her son, "I am sorry for my son's intrusion. My name is, Sakura Konishi, and I am the person in charge of this exhibit. I hope my son has not been troubling your daughter."

Aiko and Oksana let the assumption go as neither one really minded.

"Everything is fine. No trouble," Aiko responded. "Can you tell us more about the tanto?"

Sakura obliged, "This particular tanto is known to be one of the few remaining tantos from the Ako incident from around the turn of the eighteenth century. That dark discoloration on the blade is said to be the blood of the samurai who took his own life along with forty-six others who gave their lives out of honor for their master."

Kyle leaned in toward Sakura and offered to shake her hand and she accepted, "You really know your stuff. My name is Kyle Morrell and this is Aiko."

"Thank you. It would be my honor to have you as my guest for this evening's event."

Aiko reached out to shake Sakura's hand, in doing so, she noticed a scar across her thumb.

Kyle, wanting to get another chance to get a better look at the displays, took advantage of the moment, "No apology needed. Thank you for your offer and we accept. It's very kind of you."

Aiko sensed a familiarity, "Did you say your name was Sakura?"

"Yes. Have we met?"

Kyle was intrigued and asked Aiko, "Do you know her?"

"Yes," Aiko replied confidently. "I am the one who gave her that scar."

Sakura seemed to know the answer before she asked, "Aiko?"

CHAPTER 8

The sun was setting just as it did yesterday about this time on the house that stood at sixteen hundred Pennsylvania Avenue but President Dalton only had one thing on his mind, unlike yesterday. Today he had a teenage daughter that may hold the key to his survival. What does one say to such a person? "Hello, I'm your father, the leader of the free world. I know we just met but I hope you can save my life."

Dalton was in the Oval Office sitting behind his desk. He wasn't looking at the notes he had on his desk that would prep him for the weekly press conference but instead, was lost in thought about the choices we make in life. He had spun his chair around and he was looking outside. He watched the clouds take on the colors of the sunset as they slowly dissolve through the spectrum of the rainbow from light to dark. It gave him a new perspective on time and how emotions were attached to colors. He could feel his thoughts changing from light to dark just like the clouds and he knew if he could reach out and grab for the clouds he would have just as many answers to his many questions. Nothing at all.

The second time his secretary knocked at the door caught his attention, "Come in."

As the door opened, Ryan Wintersteen, the head of the FBI walked in and greeted his commander in chief. The two of them took a seat opposite each other on the matching couches that occupied the settee area in the middle of the Oval Office.

Dalton had only one thought at this moment, "Why wasn't I told about this?"

Wintersteen did his best to answer as direct, "You yourself asked us to keep it under wraps, Sir."

"You'd better have a better explanation."

"Remember those photos you asked us to bury around the time of your election and all the information that we gathered along with them? Well, in our investigation we found out the woman in the photograph, Karina Pankov, had a daughter that we were able to identify as yours through a DNA sample."

"Are you sure about this? Where did you get the DNA?"

"We had Pankov under surveillance and we were able to acquire the DNA once we knew where they were taking the girl for hospital visits."

"So, you're sure?"

"Yes, Sir. Her code name is Red Butterfly."

Dalton took a moment to try and piece together the images that were flashing through his mind as he walked over to the wet-bar and poured the two of them a drink. "What is her real name?"

"Oksana."

"So that would make her about fifteen or so. You know where she is?"

"Portland Oregon."

Another knock at the door reminded Dalton he wasn't dreaming.

Dalton couldn't even hear himself think let alone hear his own words as he said, "Come in."
The door opened and his secretary, Jennifer Lawson, came in but he knew she wouldn't do that so he must have said something. The next thing he knew he had an envelope in hand.

The secretary wasn't even sure if the President heard her, "This is the information you were waiting for, Sir."

After a long pause, "Thank you, Jennifer."

Wintersteen waited for the secretary to close the door behind her before he asked, "The results from Dr. Riggs?"

Dalton opened the envelope, "Yes." Dalton found himself pacing around the couch as he read over the results, "It looks like neither one of my kids is a close enough match to be a bone marrow donor."

"Is there any other treatment that can be done that doesn't need a donor?"

"Riggs says for the best results we need a donor with an eighty-five percent match or better and to do this as soon as possible."

Wintersteen knew what had to be done and broke the ice, "Sir."

"Yes, I know. We're going to need to find the girl to see if she is a match. Ryan, this can't get out. Bring her directly to Walter Reed Hospital. We can control the narrative on this a lot better that way."

"Yes, Sir." Wintersteen went to his wireless communication device, "Give me the file on Red Butterfly."

****

One of the local restaurants just outside the George Anthony studios, called the Hizou, had converted its normally Asian American menu to a more traditional Japanese style for the duration of the current exhibit.

Everyone had just finished their meals when the check came and was set down between Kyle and Sakura. Aiko smiled as Sakura took the leather pouch from Kyle's hand, "Not on your life. Let me have that. You are my guest."

Oksana watched as Zen finished his last yakisoba noodle with one loud slurp.

Sakura added her credit card to the leather folder then asked for Aiko's phone. As Aiko did not have hers with her, Kyle offered his.

Sakura typed in her number, "There, now we have each other's numbers and I expect you to keep in touch."

"I'm sure we will, Kyle replied. "So, tell me more about how Aiko gave you that scar."

Aiko gave her explanation first, "It was an accident."

Sakura felt it needed more clarity, "An accident? When Aiko and I were in the orphanage together, we also trained together. Aiko was one of the best because she never held back."

Oksana needed to know more, "Sword training?"

Sakura turned toward Oksana, "Oh, no. We were too young for swords. This was from a bokuto."

Oksana was thrilled to know what that was, "I have one of those. Aiko is training me. I can't wait to train with the sword."

Zen was just a little older than Oksana, already a black belt, but still a teen searching for his own identity, "I have been training with a sword for over two years now."

Oksana knew what Aiko was about to say because it was one of her mantras, "To learn is to understand more than what is being taught and to know its proper use."

Zen was still trying to impress Oksana, "My sensei is the best. She says I am her best student and one day I will be a master sensei myself."

Oksana eyes rolled back as if to say, Aiko, please don't embarrass me with another one of your mantras. It was too late.

"Do not rush to be the master or the master will never appear."

Sakura saw that Zen was coming on a little too strong so she agreed with Aiko, "You better listen to Aiko. I was in a hurry to be the best."

Sakura raised her hand so both Zen and Oksana could see the scar across her thumb, "Even a wooden training sword can hurt you, especially if the one wielding it cracks you across the hand."

Aiko put her hand on Oksana's shoulder to stop her from telling anymore, "I…"

Kyle could sense the challenges as well as the caution being tested, "And look at you now, Sakura, you're a head curator of a rare antiquities firm."

"The company I work for is very diversified. This show is a fund raiser to help fund a project we are very close to getting off the ground. We just need a few more pieces to fall into place and will be a great find for our company."

"A find?" Kyle inquired, "What are you looking for?"

"It is called, The Monarch Moon."

Aiko had to interject, "That is just a legend."

After a pause that prompted more, Oksana had to ask, "What is the Monarch Moon?"

Sakura was ready with a reply as if waiting for the question, "Aiko can tell you. She is named after it, the legend itself."

All eyes seem to focus on Aiko and in that moment Aiko felt as if she had been set up by her friend to tell the story, "When we were growing up in the orphanage, Sakura and I would hear stories of a legendary yellow sapphire called the Monarch Moon."

Oksana was confused, "I thought your name meant, beloved?"

Sakura was eager to have Aiko continue the story so she was happy to lead with another prompt, "That's correct. But the sapphire was part of a lost treasure that went down on a ship a couple of hundred years ago, off the coast of Japan."

Aiko felt the nudge from her friend to continue, "It is thought to believe that the ship was a Spanish galleon called the AMADA. In Spanish, that means, beloved. The legend goes that its cargo was on its way through the silk route bringing the finest of jewels and gold when it was hijacked by pirates."

Now it was Kyle's turn to prompt Sakura, "And it's never been found?"

"Lost in the Sea of Japan. The story goes, in a thick fog it hit something and it went down never to be heard of again. That is until years later an old man on his death bed told a story of a pirate that was on that ship, and was able to tread water for hours until he was picked up by some fishermen."

Kyle looked at Zen and Oksana and in a spooky voice responded, "And so the legend began."

Sakura said in a solid tone, as of a matter of fact, "It is more than just a legend."

"How can you be so sure?" Kyle asked.

"We are in possession of some information that can confirm the man's story."

Kyle being all about the facts, "Then why haven't you gone after it?"

"Over the years the few who knew of the wreck had taken its location to their grave. This is the best lead we have substantiated as being authentic."

"What kind of information?"

"Clues."

"Clues?"

"Hidden, authenticated, clues, actually."

Oksana didn't bother holding back the light that went off in her mind, "The yakuza tattoos."

Everyone's attention went right over to Oksana. With that simple, honest, direct answer of what she figured out told Sakura, Kyle, and Aiko that they were all in possession of information that was once hidden and was now in the open.

Oksana hadn't realized what she had done, "What?"

Kyle's phone rang and he took the call, "Yes, this is Morrell."

Aiko looked at her friend from her past as if this accidental rendezvous wasn't that much of an accident.

Kyle hung up the call and with a concerned glance to Aiko, "We have to go."

There was a bit of tension in the air as everyone stood to say their goodbyes. Aiko had to wonder if Sakura could sense the lack of trust in her words, "Thank you, Sakura, for dinner. You have been most kind."

"We have each other's number and will have to stay in touch."

Kyle knew those words felt like, "We can track you," and he didn't like the feeling.

Once Kyle had Aiko and Oksana cleared from the dining area he tried to rush them to the exit.

Aiko felt the sense of urgency, "Who was that on the phone?"

"It was Detective DeMint. He said his file on us was just flagged. He said the FBI is coming for Oksana."

Upon exiting the Hizou restaurant, Aiko could feel Kyle's grip of her hand as a protective one but also felt the danger. She tried not to give Oksana the same feeling as she had Oksana's hand firmly in her grasp with her other hand.

Aiko didn't have time to ask Kyle about slowing down when suddenly, the rush across the pavement came to a dead stop.

Aiko felt Oksana wrap her arms around her in fear as the three of them were now encircled by four FBI agents.

Sakura exited the restaurant just in time to see her childhood friend being escorted to a black van that was waiting at the curb. She watched as the door closed and they drove away. Knowing how the dinner conversation went, she had to wonder, how much did they really know?

CHAPTER 9

Outside the Walter Reed Hospital in Bethesda Maryland, sat a couple of cars from the President's motorcade and as two more cars arrived, agents secured the area.

It was the middle of the night so foot traffic was low and made it easier for the agents to escort Kyle, Aiko, and Oksana into the hospital with little fanfare. Once inside, two agents escorted Oksana, along with a nurse, into one elevator.

Aiko saw a little fear and anxiety on Oksana's face but assured her, "Everything will be okay." The doors closed. Another two agents escorted Kyle and Aiko into a second elevator.

Aiko sat as Kyle paced in and about the secured lobby. The lounge was very modern in the sense it really tried to use all of the space to make you feel relaxed. The space contained small palm trees as well as beautiful green ferns. The neon lighting was on a dimmer and varied throughout the day accordingly. There was a couch with pillows and two chairs that looked and felt very comfortable for those times when waiting was the hardest part. The coffee table had the latest issues of People Magazine and an issue of today's USA Today Newspaper, not the ones from six months ago.

In the distance, two agents stood watch as Aiko walked over to the window where Kyle had paused to see if he could tell if the sun was coming up soon. Although it was a short trip across the states, Kyle didn't handle jetlag very well. He didn't get much sleep on the plane and never bothered changing his watch so maybe that was it.

Maybe it was that he knew what he was feeling. Like a protective father worried about the welfare of his child standing next to the woman he loved.

Aiko could feel it too.

Across the lobby a door opened to one of the examination rooms. A nurse walked Oksana out and headed her in the direction of the lobby. Oksana ran away from the nurse and into Kyle and Aiko's arms.

Oksana was scared and Kyle tried to reassure her, "Are you alright, Oksana?"

"Yes. I'm fine." Oksana showed Kyle and Aiko the Band-Aid on the inside of her elbow, "They just took a couple vials of my blood."

The door to the exam room that Oksana had just came from opened once again, a doctor holding a collection tray stepped out, and was joined by an agent who escorted the doctor down the hallway.

Kyle began to follow the doctor down the hall, "Doctor, can you please tell us, what's going on?"

Before Kyle could exit the lobby, a Secret Service agent asked him to remain in the lobby. A second agent made a call over his wireless communication device.

Kyle tried to stay calm and rely on his cop instincts that everything would be okay, but the jetlag wasn't going to let it be. "When is someone going to tell us, what's going on?"

A familiar voice caught his attention, "How about now?" said the President.

President Dalton approached Kyle as two of his personal agents stopped and held back to observe. Dalton extended his hand, "Hello, Detective Morrell."

Kyle was tired but knew he wasn't dreaming, "Mr. President."

Kyle turned his attention to formally introduce Aiko and Oksana even though he figured he already knew who they were, "This is Aiko and Oksana."

Dalton shook both their hands but took a little more time with Oksana as he took a good look into her eyes, "It's a pleasure to meet you both."

Dalton put out his hand and suggested they all take a seat, "I'm sorry for the greeting and circumstances in Portland but the secrecy in this matter is vital."

"You don't want the secret to get out you are my father?" Oksana replied.

Everyone was taken aback by Oksana's bold statement.

Dalton gave Oksana the same respect, "You may not believe me but it wasn't until a short time ago that I even knew of the possibility of your existence."

"Do you remember my mother?"

Dalton motioned to one of the agents who handed him a file.

"A few days ago, I was handed this file. I've had a chance to go over it thoroughly. I can't tell you everything that happened for security reasons but I can tell you that if I had known, things would have been different. Very different."

Dalton set the file down on the table in front of him. Everyone's attention seemed to be locked onto the file. There, on the tab on the side of the file, was the name…Red Butterfly.

Everyone had questions but Aiko needed to ask, "There has to be something more to all this. Why now?"

"I don't want to get too far ahead of ourselves, but if it turns out that Oksana is my daughter, there is a possibility that we can help each other."

Once again, everyone in the group eyed each other, knowing that each question answered only raised more questions.

Dalton did not want to go into any more depth until he had conclusive results from the blood tests, "It's been a very long day for you, so why don't we all get some rest, and we can meet again tomorrow. Two of my men will get you settled into a secure location and the next time we see each other we'll have more to go on. How does that sound?"

Kyle wanted more but knew now was not the time, "Sounds like you're putting us up in a safe house for the night."

"It's for your own security and as far as anyone knows, you're not here."

* * * * * * * *

Sakura was in bed asleep when she heard a ping on her phone. The dim light from the face of her iPhone showed she had a text. The heading on the text read, Lost and Found. She opened the text and there was a photo of the White House.

Sakura sat up in bed and hit redial on one of the latest calls. There was an answer but no voice on the other end as Sakura gave out the long-awaited news, "Yes, I'm calling about the item you were interested in. It looks like we have located one. In fact, we have three of them." After a short pause, Sakura continued, "Washington DC."

CHAPTER 10

After getting some rest, a shower, and a hearty breakfast, Kyle, Aiko, and Oksana were once again in the same secured lobby of the Walter Reed Hospital at the request of the President.

Although the circumstances had changed, it did still feel like a dream despite having had a Secret Service escort first thing in the morning. It was a nice touch if it was truly a dream.

Kyle sipped his coffee while Aiko stood by a window taking in as much sun on her skin as she could. The warmth reminded her of the safety of Kyle's arms.

Oksana sat anxiously waiting to talk with the man who was not only the President of the United States but if the blood test confirmed it, her father. Oksana had the flash drive in her hand and her restlessness couldn't be contained. She was flipping it through her fingers like a drummer whirling his drum stick through his fingers before cracking the snare one more time.

Kyle walked up behind Aiko and put his arms around her, "Do you think we asked for too much?"

Before Aiko could answer, Oksana had a question, "Do you think I should have asked for a car? I am going to be able to drive soon."

One of the President's Secret Service agents entered the lobby just a minute ahead of the President, saw the room was secure, and went to his wireless mic, "It's clear."

A moment later Dalton arrived holding a small box in his hand. He took a seat next to Oksana and handed her the gift, "Before you open the box, it's my understanding you have brought the flash drive, and if what you say is true, I am very grateful for you telling us about it."

"Oh, so it is true? You were being blackmailed and never knew about me?"

"I give you my word, Oksana."

Oksana had so many emotions running through her she had hardly any control in her hands to open the gift. The box was one of those hinged boxes like what a Rolex watch comes in. Once she had the lid open she saw the most beautiful stick-pin, it was a red butterfly. As if in a trance, Oksana handed over the flash drive without taking her eyes off the red butterfly, as its red crystals that made up the wings seemed to flutter as the light reflected off them.

Oksana nodded as the President thanked her for the flash drive.

In turn, Dalton handed the drive to one of the agents who walked over to a nearby table and loaded the flash drive into a laptop.

Kyle and Aiko knew from Dalton's expression that the blood test had confirmed that he was in fact Oksana's biological father.

They watched the way Dalton looked at Oksana, that he was okay with the results, and was going to do what was best for Oksana.

Oksana closed the fancy box with the stick-pin still inside and placed it on the coffee table. She then reached into her pocket and slowly removed an object she kept hidden in her hand as if she was still deciding if she wanted to give it up and return it to its rightful owner. She opened her hand and showed the President his flag-pin from when he was a Senator. Oksana handed it to him and he looked on the back and saw his four-digit code proving it was his and just one more identifying confirmation that Oksana was his too.

"Yes, this was my pin."

"My mother gave it to me and told me one day it would have a special meaning."

"Then you should keep it."

"It was never mine to keep."

"I'll tell you what," the President removed his current flag-pin from his lapel. "You can have this one." The President attached the flag-pin to Oksana's collar.

"There. Now you are officially a member of this administration."

Oksana showed Aiko and Kyle her new pin. President Dalton realized that flag-pin meant more to her then the red butterfly stick-pin and he was okay with that.

Dalton had a gift for Kyle and Aiko as well, "We're working on the papers for citizenship for Oksana and for you, Aiko, that will give you dual citizenship for here and Japan. But in the meantime, I have these for you."

One of the Secret Service agents handed Dalton a medium size manila envelope and whispered something in his ear.

Dalton not only had gifts but more questions, "In here are three passports. One for each of you. I have a number of questions for you Aiko."

"Yes."

"It may be of a sensitive matter."

"You can speak freely. I have nothing to hide."

"In doing our background check, we discovered your family has a business that is a front for human trafficking."

Kyle tried to get ahead of the question as not to put Aiko through anymore of this line of questioning, "That was in Portland and that was shut down six months ago."

Dalton continued with the facts, "Yes. Red Sun Exports was shut down but according to our findings, what was going on there was just an extension of Masato Enterprises of Japan."

Aiko was confused, "I am unaware of such a business."

"I believe you, Aiko. What can you tell me about, Kamiko Masato?"

Now, not only was Aiko confused but so was Kyle.

Aiko thought for a moment, "I do not know that name."

"Your father was Ichiro Masato correct?"

"Yes."

"According to our findings she was your father's younger sister, the sole owner of Masato enterprises, and that would make her, your aunt."

"I only knew of my father, Ichiro, last year. I was raised in an orphanage until he took me out and gave me a life and training as a samurai geisha."

That piqued Dalton's attention, "A samurai geisha?"

"Yes." Aiko saw the surprise in Dalton from her answer and now had a question of her own, "I don't want to sound ungrateful but why now? Why, after all this time, do you want to claim Oksana as your daughter?"

"I may be her biological father but it looks like you and Mr. Morrell are doing a fine job raising her."

Oksana felt torn but relieved, "So, I can stay with them?"

Dalton could see the affection Oksana had for Kyle and Aiko, "I do not see why not. There will be some paperwork involved if that is what you want."

Kyle needed to know more, "So then why all the cloak and dagger?"

Dalton had more than the results of Oksana being his daughter but the confirmation of his own bloodwork, "The truth is, I have been diagnosed with leukemia."

Kyle followed up, "So you needed to test Oksana to see if she was a match?"

"The doctors say the best and most effective way to go about finding a cure is a bone marrow donor. I have two other children and as it turns out, they are not a close enough match. Nothing changes. Aiko and Oksana will still get their citizenship, you'll still get to keep your passports, and Oksana will still have the option to be with you. Being a bone marrow donor is a big decision and you should take some time to think about it."

Oksana didn't hesitate, "I'll do it."

CHAPTER 11

The large room was about the same space as a two-story open loft. If one could have their own private museum, this was it. The bottom half was made of brick and the upper half was crafted from timbers made of redwood. The windows were protected by hand crafted shutters, both inside and out. The room was naturally temperature controlled like a wine cellar from its thick rock walls. All the windows were bolted from the inside for privacy and helped with security. The interior lighting that was installed was designed to highlight the artifacts on display.

Most everything in the room was one of a kind. There were no price tags on any of the items as nothing was for sale. Although, if they were, this room alone would rival any high-end museum. What made these artifacts so special was they were stolen and no price could equal the lives that were lost to obtain them.

The space contained three rectangular tables arranged in a U shape. Multiple priceless artifacts were laid out for maintenance and cataloging. One in particular was off to the side away from the others. This one was in a large three by four-foot glass case and contained a human pelt with an elaborate yakuza tattoo.

The Yakuza, or Japanese mafia, have some of the most detailed and brightly colored tattoos ever seen. Japan once had a ban on tattoos so the yakuza would end their tattoos above the ankle and wrist, and never had them on the face, or neck or down the middle of the chest so the tattoos could be easily hidden by their clothing.

The method the yakuza once used to apply their tattoos was not a modern one, and is called "horimono." Its technique was done manually by hand with a stick with needles at the end usually in a bundle. This technique was very painful and expensive, and since the yakuza cover most of their body with the tattoo it could take up to thirty years to finish and can cost anywhere from twenty to fifty thousand dollars.

A pair of woman's hands passed over the artisan's work. She was wearing a set of white gloves to keep the artwork as pristine as possible. The way her hand moved as it slowly hovered just above the art was as if she was caressing the work without ever touching it. Her appreciation was an addiction.

There was a knock at the door. A man entered carrying a briefcase. He set the case down, opened it, then removed an item that was wrapped in white linen. He handed the item to the woman.

The woman's gloved hand carefully opened the linen and removed the item. She held it up to the light to get a better look.

It was the piece, known as the legend, that was taken from the secret drawer of the stand that displayed the Guardian. The one Aiko and Oksana almost lost their lives over.

The woman took it over and set it down next to the large glass encased frame containing the piece of human pelt. She removed a key from her pocket and unlocked the case and slid open the frame. She then placed the legend up next to a small gap on the side of the pelt where it seemed to be an almost perfect fit.

Her hand went back and forth from the legend to different spots on the tattoo and made notes from her interpretation of the clues hidden within the tattoo.

In the end, the note read: Monāku mūn no gādian, Guardian of the Monarch Moon.

CHAPTER 12

Just a few miles south of the Walter Reed Hospital, about ten minutes down the one ninety, was the small town of Somerset. A nice place to have a secured location suitable as a safe house for Kyle, Aiko and Oksana. The house was close enough to freeway access so with one word from the President they could be recalled quickly.

Oksana had been playing with a box of dominos. She had put most of them on edge when one fell and, in turn, the others laid down in sequence before she could stop them. Aiko began to help her set them back up.

"Which one are you, Oksana?"

"What do you mean?"

"Once you have them all arranged, which one are you?"

"I still don't understand."

"You always have a choice in how you choose to set up the dominoes. Then what?"

"I knock them down."

"So, I ask you again. Which one are you?"

Oksana knew this was more than just about the dominos and wanted to get the answer right so she looked hard at all of the dominos then to Aiko. Oksana was looking for a clue from Aiko but realized the answer was within herself.

She also knew that Aiko wanted her to find it on her own. Aiko saw the wheels start to turn in Oksana's mind and left her alone to find the answer.

Kyle was in the bedroom and was looking at the edge of the katana's hilt. He turned the edge against the light so he could see it better. The ancient text still didn't make any sense to him.

Kyle heard a knock at the door. He slid the sword all the way in its scabbard and tossed it on the bed.

Kyle went into the dining area as one of the Secret Service agents was dropping off an order of Japanese take-out. Kyle asked if they would like some dinner as they had ordered a full family sized meal. The agent declined as Aiko began to prepare the plates. Kyle took a seat at the table as Oksana set up the silverware for Kyle, chopsticks for Aiko, and a set of both for herself.

Oksana had been thinking about what Aiko said and thought she would ask Kyle for his opinion, "If you set up a long line of dominos on the edge knowing if one fell, they all fell, which one would you be?"

Kyle knew he was being probed for another pop quiz from Aiko and sure enough when he looked to Aiko to find out, she was already looking over her shoulder at Kyle.

He thought about it for a second, "Hmmm, I'm not sure. What are your thoughts?"

"Well, at times I think I am in the middle somewhere."

"How's that?"

Oksana glanced at Aiko before giving her answer as if wondering if her response was what Aiko was looking for, "I am no longer a child and have become a student learning from Aiko to become a better version of myself, which will manifest itself in the future. So, I am in the middle."

Kyle was impressed with Oksana's answer and could tell she had put a lot of thought into it, "Very good, Oksana. That sounded pretty good to me."

Kyle looked to Aiko for his own approval but it seemed that was not the answer Aiko was looking for. Kyle once again took a moment to find a solution to the problem then crossed his fingers, "How about, if you are in the middle you are neither a leader or a follower. If you are the last domino, you will be always waiting on others to tell you what to do, and if the first domino you will be in control of your own actions."

Both Kyle and Oksana looked to Aiko for approval and got nothing. Aiko just turned and finished preparing the dinner. Kyle and Oksana took that as a win and high-fived each other.

Although Aiko's serving portions were small, Kyle was very appreciative of Aiko's choice for dinner. It reminded him of a beef bento from one of the local food carts downtown but Kyle didn't dare say that to Aiko. Instead he was thankful she gave him a healthier portion, "I think this is becoming one of my favorite meals."

"Thank you, Kyle-son. This is Sukiyaki with crisp vegetables served with white rice. When I was a child this was one of my favorites and I knew when I got older I would make it for my family."

Everyone caught what Aiko said as the first time she had referred to the three of them as family. It sounded all right to Kyle and Oksana so they didn't comment and just smiled at each other.

Oksana giggled as she got a kick out of the way Aiko referred to Kyle and mimicked, "Yes, Kyle-son. Now all you have to do is learn how to use a pair of chopsticks."

Even that brought a smile to Aiko as she was just thinking the same thing.

There was another knock at the door. Kyle must have thought the Secret Service agents had changed their minds about the offer. Kyle joked, "Come on in! We have extra!"

Kyle heard the door open and could sense the two men approaching him from behind as he started take a bite of his meal. "Can we get you guys something?"

The two men came closer to the table.

Oksana saw a tattoo near the wrist on one of the men from under his ill-fitted jacket. The tattoo reminded her of one of the men who attacked her at Kyle's house.

Oksana immediately felt the danger, "Kyle!"

It was too late. The two Asian men were on them and one had Kyle at bay with a knife to his throat. The other, shorter man, stood behind Oksana with his hands on her shoulders.

Aiko was calm, "What do you want?"

The man who stood over Oksana with the ill-fitted jacket was definitely yakuza and from his almost perfect English, seemed to be very well-educated, "The Guardian. Where is it?"

Aiko responded quickly as if to try to hide her lie, "It is not here."

The shorter man kept one hand on Oksana as he reached into his pocket and tossed a business card onto Aiko's plate, "Bring it to this address. You have seventy-two hours or the girl dies."

Since the time the man had put his hands on her shoulders, Oksana had her hands under the table resting on her lap. In her left hand, she was holding a fork.

Kyle was sitting just to the left of Oksana and she was able to poke Kyle in the knee with her fork.

Aiko was doing her best at trying to appear to be cooperating, "You're going to have to give us more time."

The man's reply was firm, "Your time has already started."

Suddenly, in a single motion, Kyle gripped the man's wrist with his left hand and pulled the knife away from his throat as he reached back with the fork in his right hand and stabbed his captor in the right thigh.

Aiko quickly stood and pulled the dining table out and to her left enabling Oksana to pull away from her captor and jump forward toward Aiko.

Aiko pushed Oksana to the floor, reached over to the table and grabbed her ceramic dinner plate. As the man who once stood behind Oksana lunged forward toward Aiko, she used the plate to slap the man hard across his face, shattering the plate into pieces.

At the same time, Kyle had stood and threw his right elbow back into the man behind him, right into his assailant's throat.

The man that stood in front of Aiko was momentarily dazed. As the man was gaining his composure, Aiko grabbed her chopsticks. As the man stumbled toward her, she took a chopstick in each hand and rested the large ends of the sticks in the base of her palms. She then took a step for leverage and shoved the sticks up inside each of the man's nostrils driving most of the nine inch wooden sticks deep into his brain.

The man stood there momentarily, dying on his feet, before he collapsed and fell to the floor.

Kyle now had two hands gripped on the man's wrist, in which he held a knife. The man drove a hard kidney punch into Kyle's lower back, buckling his knees. In return, Kyle raised his right heel and kicked a fork that was still protruding from the man's right thigh. This momentary jolt of pain was enough for Kyle to gain the advantage and free the knife from his assailant. Kyle regripped the knife, spun around, and put the blade's edge to the man's throat.

Kyle had one question, "Who sent you?"

"I did," Sakura replied.

For Kyle and Aiko, the nightmare continued as they looked over and saw Sakura flanked by two more yakuza. Each of them were holding a gun, one at Kyle, and the other at Aiko. Kyle got a glimpse beyond the intruders; their Secret Service detail lay dead outside on the porch.

The assailant in front of Kyle took his knife back, grabbed Oksana, and led her over to Sakura. Sakura reached down, pulled the fork that was still protruding from the man's thigh, and tossed it back in Kyle's direction.

The tone in Sakura's voice was cold and without emotion, "Seventy-two hours."

Sakura and her henchmen left with Oksana, leaving Kyle and Aiko stunned.

CHAPTER 13

The elevator door pinged, then opened on the secured floor of the hospital. One of the Secret Service agents came off first followed by Aiko who was carrying the Guardian, who was followed by Kyle and the second Secret Service agent. As Aiko and Kyle crossed over into the lounge, the agents stayed back at a distance.

The bay windows that allowed the sun's rays to tend to the vegetation in the room also warmed the lounge area.

Aiko walked up to President Dalton who, with a wave of his hand, offered Aiko and Kyle a seat on the couch as he took one of the end chairs. Aiko set the katana down in the middle of the table. The detailed craftsmanship of the sword did not compare to its true value.

Aiko had wiped away the blood and pencil shavings from the side of the hilt. No one else knew of the secret that it held.

Dalton felt the honor in Aiko's words, "The sword is one of three that were commissioned from my ancestor who was a master swordsman by the name of Masamune."

"Why do they want it so bad?"

"There is a set of three and I can only assume whoever wants this one, has the other two."

"Do you know who they are?"

"No, but whoever they are, they're willing to kill for them."

Dalton picked up the sword, felt its weight, and was admiring the detail as he asked, "What's it worth?"

Dalton once again felt Aiko's words, "At this moment, Oksana's life."

Kyle needed to let Dalton know he was willing to do anything to get Oksana back, "The people who want this took Oksana to make sure we would deliver it to them on time."

Kyle handed the business card that was left on Aiko's plate with the name, Marine Science Technologies, to Dalton.

Kyle did not let go of the card as Dalton took a hold of the other end to make sure he had his attention. "We now have less than seventy-two hours to get this sword to this address."

Dalton did a double take as he read the address on the business card, "This is in Sapporo Japan." Dalton turned to one of his agents and handed him the business card, "Run this." Dalton began to pace the room, not only as the President in deep thought over a controversial ballot measure, but now as a father having to make a life-and-death decision that could not only affect his daughter's life, but his own.

Kyle felt his dilemma, "Aiko and I have already discussed the options and if you want to keep this out of the press, you cannot use our Embassy in Japan or send in men of your own because if they see you coming, they will kill Oksana."

Aiko continued to plead their case, "With your help, I would like to go with Kyle to Japan and trade the sword for Oksana."

The Secret Service agent returned with the business card and handed it back to Dalton.

"What could you find out?"

"Marine Science Technologies is a shell company that is owned by Masato Enterprises, making the owner of record, Kamiko Masato," the agent replied.

****

The private Gulfstream G650 jet with its logo, Marine Science Technologies, was flying high above the Pacific Ocean.

Oksana was looking out the window at the clouds below as the sun's rays had painted a golden fleece over them. She felt the slight vibration of the wing's flaps just as the pilot altered the plane's course to the new heading. She watched as the flaps came back to their original position and the plane leveled off. Beyond the clouds, she saw the Pacific Ocean peeking through the clouds at times, as it stretched out all the way to the horizon, and let her mind wonder, wishing she was anywhere else but here.

Oksana's meal sat on her tray hardly touched.

Oksana's mind was so far away she barely heard Sakura, "You should eat something. It's a long trip to Japan."

"I'm not hungry."

"How about a movie or a book?"

Oksana did not answer. She just continued to look out the large round window.

A steward approached holding the phone, "Ms. Konishi, you have a phone call."

Sakura took the phone and walked a few rows down the middle of the cabin but Oksana could still hear her end of the conversation, "Yes, everything is on schedule and you should have the Guardian within seventy-two hours."

Sakura took a glance back at Oksana who still seemed to be lost looking out at the clouds and continued, "We will have complete control of the location and the exchange."

Oksana had to hold in the secret she realized she now had when she heard Sakura say over the phone, "I do not think they know the true value of the Guardian."

CHAPTER 14

President Dalton entered the lounge area expecting to see Kyle and Aiko but only saw Secret Service agents. He looked at the agent in charge who gave him a nod with his head indicating they were in the nearest exam room; the closest thing to privacy as they could get.

Dalton took a stroll over to the window and looked out over the city's landscape as he often did to help ease his mind. He'd imagined what it would be like to take a long walk through the countryside all alone, to feel the pine needles below his feet under his cowboy boots that he liked to wear when he could, and to smell the crisp air and watch a leaf ride the wind without a care. He knew those days were from what seemed like long ago and he may never see them again, but he liked to dream one day he would have the chance once again. It gave him hope.

Kyle and Aiko were talking privately in one of the examination rooms.

Aiko couldn't help but feel responsible and does not want to jeopardize anyone else, "I need to do this alone. I cannot ask you to risk your life for mine. If we both go, they will have the advantage."

"There is no way you are going without me."

"This, is a family matter. My family."

"And you and Oksana are my family."

Aiko wanted to believe him but her look said differently.

Aiko's heart was torn, "I still do not understand, why are you willing to risk everything for me?"

"Because I'm hoping one day you will."

There was a light knock at the door and an agent entered, "The President is ready to see you."

Kyle and Aiko joined Dalton.

Like before, answers seemed to lead to more questions and Dalton had another one, "We've been going over the flash drive Oksana gave to us. Are you aware that one of the programs it contains is still active?"

Kyle bit, "What does it do?"

"The file is a complete list of all the girls Ichiro Masato has sold over the last year and their location. We're not sure how many yet or how it's tracking, but it is still tracking."

Aiko knew, "He has implanted each of the girls with a chip."

Aiko showed Dalton a small scar on the inner part of her arm, "He even had one in me until Kyle removed it."

Dalton felt confident with all the resources he had at his disposal they would be able to match the frequency and start finding the girl's locations, but at the same time, he knew there was a catch, "I guess how many we can track down will depend on how long the internal battery will last."

Kyle was ready to get started, "Let Aiko and I both go to Japan and do the exchange for Oksana. While we are there, we can do some recon on this and find out if there is a connection to what went on in Portland at Masato Enterprises."

As President his hands were tied, "We just lost two agents and that makes this as federal as it gets. I can't put you both in harm's way."

Aiko knew she needed to stand her ground, "We are already involved."

Kyle took advantage of the door that was open, "They are expecting us. We are already in play. We are the best chance you have at getting Oksana back."

Dalton knew Kyle was not the type to just sit back and it made his decision easier, "Kyle, you are a detective with the Portland police, correct?"

"Yes, Sir."

"So, you are familiar with ICE?"

"Ice?" Aiko interjected.

Kyle acknowledged to both Dalton and Aiko, "Yeah, one of the things they do is to investigate human trafficking."

Dalton confirmed, "Yes, the Immigration and Customs Enforcement. They fall under Homeland Security. They investigate cases both here domestically and abroad. I'm thinking I can give you the resources you will need to help get Oksana back safely."

Feeling encouraged, Kyle took Aiko by the hand.

"It looks like you and Aiko are our best source of intel at this time, and time is what we have very little of."

Kyle was humbled, "I don't know what to say."

Dalton was looking for an affirmative answer, "Say you'll do it before I change my mind."

Kyle knew risking his own life was one thing but he knew Aiko would not just sit back and wait, "To pull this off we are going to have to do this on our own."

Aiko didn't miss a beat, "We will have to fly commercial and use our own money as not to draw attention."

Kyle kept the demands coming, "In fact, we're going to need you to redo our passports and back date them. Maybe doctor them up a little with trips to Canada and Mexico to make them look used so they won't stand out."

Dalton could see everyone was already committed, "You're going to need money for expenses."

Kyle didn't hesitate, "Cash is good."

CHAPTER 15

Some of the ships that made their way through the Sea
of Japan passed through the quiet canal district of Niigata,
which was located near the mouth of the Shinano River,
which served as one of the main ports of call for Japanese
trade. Tonight, the air was still. One building in particular
was sealed off and sound proofed from the elements and
stood out from the rest. When everyone else was gathering
from the day's events for dinner, this building was quiet,
always quiet. The locals knew to stay away and not talk to
anyone about anything that they may have seen or heard
concerning this well guarded brick building. It had a solid
base and the upper half had stations where men were posted
in the shadows. No one really knew what went on there but
the ones who did know, their lives depended on their
silence.

Inside, in part of the loft that was well insulated, two
cash counting bank machines were running one-hundred
dollar bills simultaneously as fast as they could be reloaded.
Next to those machines, was another, counting Yen. On any
given day, the market could change, but at the current
market rate the exchange was about one-hundred and twelve
Japanese Yen to the U.S. Dollar as compared to the
Canadian trading at one point three to the dollar.

The man running the machines was wearing a lab coat with no pockets. This was a standard practice when handling currency to avoid anyone with sticky fingers, and even less common sense, to want to pocket a few for themselves.

The auditor removed both denominations of cash from each of the machines, adjusted his glasses, then made notations in his ledgers. He then transferred the dollar amounts into a computer next to corresponding names. When he was done, he printed out a report.

In the next room, the woman in the white gloves was methodically going over the tattoo which once belonged to a yakuza warrior. The human pelt had given up a few secrets, but not enough.

The auditor entered the room and set the final tally report on the corner of one of the tables nearest to her, "Today's numbers." He could barely get the words out without breaking a sweat. Although he came highly recommended, he knew the consequences if his work was less than satisfactory.

The woman didn't flinch. Not even a thank you for her new assistant who was trying very hard to show his loyalty ever since taking over for the last accountant. A man who lost more than his hands for over stepping his bounds when he removed a diamond from the safe, even if only to get a better look at it. Before he could replace it, Kamiko didn't ask any questions, she just removed a sword from the display stand and without hesitation, removed his hands.

Her focus was still on the tattoo. She had her finger tip over a picture of a yellow butterfly in a circle. She made a notation in her notes, Guardian of the Monarch Moon. Her notes showed a big space between two sets of notes. She drew out three lines in that space indicating she was missing three items.

The woman noticed the auditor tilting his head as he tried to get a better look at the tattoo. The auditor then did a double take when he realized she was watching him.

The auditor may have felt out of place but he also noticed something else that was in place, "Excuse me for staring."

"What is it?"

The auditor did not to touch the pelt but pointed very closely at a design, "It's interesting the use of that color of orange. That color is known as, kinjiki. Yet I see it is used in three places."

"Yes. The forbidden color. Do you know the history?"

"Just what I've heard. A ranking system of social hierarchy. It was used for top ranking government officials and the high priest."

"Yes, well done, Koji-san. What a perfect way to hide a message. Only someone with such knowledge would ever notice the connection."

They both took a better look at the tattoo. Koji pointed out three images within the tattoo; a man in an orange robe committing seppuku, an orange tanken, and scabbard with a half-drawn katana.

Koji, as well as the woman, felt he might be onto something and she allowed him to continue, "Could the katana be The Guardian?"

The woman ran her hand from picture to picture. She retraced her outline once again with her finger-tip realizing she was forming a perfect triangle between the images. She then moved her finger to the center of those three objects converging on the symbol for the Monarch Moon.

She had made another discovery, "The orange tanken, or dagger, is pointing to the symbol of the Monarch Moon." She looked to Koji, "And what is Japanese word for dagger?"

His realization, "Tanto."

The woman went to her notes and wrote the word, tanto, in the first space and then went back to the tattoo and pointed to the man in orange robe next to a geisha who both had a hand on the same sword, "Which blade is known as the companion sword?"

Realization number two for the auditor, "The wakizashi."
Even before she heard his answer she was already writing in the word, wakizashi, and her notes in the second blank space.

She then referred back to the tattoo and pointed to the sword that was half-drawn from the orange scabbard, "The Guardian."

The woman filled in the third blank with the word, katana. She reran the scenario as she retraced her finger-tip once again from image to image forming the triangle.

She now saw what was there the whole time, "They form a perfect triangle and in the middle of that triangle, the legend, the Monarch Moon.

"So, what these images are saying is, there is something about this set of swords that will lead us to the treasure."

A determination underscored the passion in her words, "I need, the Guardian."

CHAPTER 16

President Dalton and Kyle were watching Aiko who was off in the corner of the private wing of the hospital slowly pacing herself through a few disciplined moves showing her control and grace with the katana that was still in its scabbard. The light coming through the windows was filtered and softened as it passed through the white curtains. The soft light highlighted Aiko and cast muted shadows on the wall.

From the naked eye, it appeared that Aiko's shadow was a heartbeat behind in mimicking Aiko's movements. The illusion was appropriate as Aiko was known as the Shadow Warrior as a child in the orphanage. When her martial arts teacher would watch her, Aiko had such concentration at a young age it made her just a bit faster at learning the techniques of hand to hand ahead of the other students.

Aiko had no life other than becoming a samurai geisha. Only a few were chosen to become both a samurai and a geisha. Being selected was an honor. It meant, in the eyes of your teachers, you showed high levels of intellect, grace, and stamina. First came high marks in education and self-discipline. Then came weaponry and becoming proficient with a katana.

One day, she was up against another girl her age and it was the first time they used fighting sticks against an opponent one on one. Both girls were very efficient with the bokutos but then Aiko overtook her opponent by slashing down across her wrist causing her to drop the bokuto.

They each had such focus neither one had noticed until the girl reached down to pick up her bokuto that Aiko had drawn blood by cutting across the outside of her thumb. With such speed and precision in technique was how Aiko became known as the Shadow Warrior.

Kyle had seen this before and leaned back toward Dalton, "You should see what she can do with the lights out."

Dalton was already impressed with what he saw so far, "I'm almost afraid to ask."

"You should be."

Dalton took a tote bag from one of his agents and handed it to Kyle, "Here's your used passports and some cash to get you started." Dalton unzipped the bag and removed a cell phone and presented it to Kyle, "We've added a few new features to your phone, one of them being a tracking device. If you lose it, we lose you."

Aiko finished her meditation and rejoined Kyle and the President.

With every moment Dalton spent in the company of Aiko he was more and more impressed and was learning not to mince any words.

"My men will take you to the airport. We've got you booked on a flight to Japan leaving in four hours. We made it look like you are catching a connecting flight from Portland."

Like Dalton, the more time she spent with him, she felt the respect was reciprocated, "Thank you, Mr. President."

Dalton smiled and gave Aiko a wink and nodded toward Kyle, "Make sure you take care of this guy."

Aiko assured him, "I will, and I will bring back your daughter."

****

Oksana was asleep in one of the six leather captain's chairs that lined each side of the aisle of the luxurious Gulfstream. The large oval windows had the sliders drawn even though it was night out. The overhead interior lighting was dimmed. The steward removed a cup of juice and tossed the rest away, "She should be asleep for about another hour."

Sakura requested, "Help me with her."
The steward sat Oksana up in her seat as the drug that was in the juice was in full effect. He then held up her left arm over her head.

Sakura pointed the tip of the injection gun just below the concave of her armpit and triggered the gun sending a microchip implant under her skin.

Sakura pulled up a file on her laptop activated application that tracks the girls. There were hundreds of red dots on the screen that covered a map of the world. She entered a new locator tracking number and the pertinent information for Oksana. Sakura zoomed in on the Pacific Ocean, over the area where their plane was flying. A new red dot appeared on the screen. Oksana.

****

On approach to Narita International Airport which is thirty-seven miles east of Tokyo Japan, the plane's glide path cut through the morning's clear blue sky that was softly painted with scattered clouds. Mt. Fuji's snow-capped mountain top was a brilliant white spectacle. Down below in the valley, the rolling hills were lined with perfectly manicured fields of many kinds of local agriculture.

Off on the horizon, unmistakable Asian architecture lined the hillside that towered over the cherry trees that were in full bloom. The blossoms skipped effortlessly through the air like pink and white snowflakes dancing hand in hand.

The jet landed and taxied past many of Narita's main airlines on route to one of Delta's gates. The international airport's major airlines were Japan Airlines, Nippon Airways and Cargo Airlines, as well as serving as the hub for Delta and United Airlines.

The interior of the airport was very impressive. Plenty of space to maneuver and very efficient.

Kyle and Aiko were in line at customs. Kyle walked up to the customs officer and handed over his passport.

The customs officer quickly flipped through the passport, "What is the purpose of your visit?"

Kyle leaned back and gestured toward Aiko, "Meeting the family."

The customs officer took a glance over Kyle's shoulder and saw Aiko, scanned the passport, then stamped the visa.

Aiko stepped to the window next and handed over her passport. The officer once again scanned the passport, stamped her visa, and handed it back to Aiko, "Welcome back to Japan and congratulations."

The officer's words confused Aiko, "Thank you?"

Aiko quickly caught up to Kyle, "What did you tell that officer?"

"That I was here to meet your family."

It took a second for Aiko to get the reference, that Kyle was implying Aiko was his fiancée. She tried, but could not hold back a smile.

At the baggage claim carousel, Kyle could see Aiko was tired and put his arm around her and drew her in. Aiko could sense him wanting to feel her next to him so she leaned and took in the comfort and warmth of his arms. She felt safe and knew her feelings for him were something she had never felt before and it was all new to her.

Every day she could feel their connection growing and redefining what she thought love was and how it was supposed to be. She was taught how to make love to a man but no one ever prepared her to be loved by a man. A man who only asked one thing of her, trust.

Aiko caught herself smiling and asked, "Why did you lie to that man and imply we were to be married?"

"Is it so hard to believe? Besides, he didn't ask any further questions and passed you right through. So, I would say it was a good cover story."

Aiko had mixed emotions, "Yes, just a story." Kyle was about to respond when Aiko turned away and grabbed her bag off the carousel then started to walk away.

Kyle grabbed his bag and followed after Aiko. Once he caught up to her, he took her bag, and rolled both pieces of luggage.

Aiko was next in line at the security baggage claim. She pulled out the claim check and handed it to the security officer who in turn handed her a tube that was about four inches around and forty inches long. The Guardian.

Kyle and Aiko were walking in silence as Kyle was looking at all the signs throughout the airport. He knew, if Aiko was not by his side, he would be lost.

Kyle realized it didn't matter where he was as long as he was with her, "Aiko."

They both stopped walking and turned toward each other.

Aiko knew by the way Kyle said her name he needed to express something more, "When we get back to the states…"

Aiko put her finger to Kyle's lips, "We need to focus on getting Oksana back, then…"

Aiko and Kyle were interrupted as two Asian men in suits each took an arm of Aiko and Kyle while a third man took their bags.

The man with their bags took command, "Do not resist or the girl will die."

Kyle needed to know, "Who sent you?"

"I did."

Kyle and Aiko recognized the voice, turned, and were both surprised to see Sakura.

Sakura continued as if she was in charge because, she was, "Actually Aiko, I was sent here by your aunt to greet you." Sakura gave it a moment to sink in before she continued, "If you would like to come this way, we have a car waiting."

CHAPTER 17

Oksana was being watched by two guards as Sakura's son, Zen, was working out in the family dojo with a bokuto. She was impressed by her surroundings. The dojo was highly-designed with interior lighting that not only lit the space, but beautiful ancient Japanese art that was commanding to be looked at and appreciated with respect.

Along with martial arts, Oksana was being taught a few Japanese words from Aiko as needed for her training. Aiko explained to Oksana a dojo was not only a place to practice and learn martial arts but a place where one went to study and learn about the truth of nature and one's existence. Like the word, dojo. Do is Japanese for a road or pathway and jo means castle or great structure. Aiko went on to explain a dojo is where one goes to find self-actualization and understanding one's true self.

Being only fifteen, Oksana had plenty of distractions and that was what Aiko was trying to relate to her about a proper dojo as a place dedicated to finding inner peace, aspirations, desires as well as delusions. What she had a hard time understanding was when Aiko would talk about examining those things she brought into the dojo herself, and learning from what was deep inside herself that were positive as well as negative.

The room had been built to use the natural light as much as possible with most of the windows facing the sun's arc across the sky for effect. The white walls that were made of paper helped to diffuse the light and gave the room an all-around even prime temperature to get the best out of one's body. The light was so perfect Oksana could clearly see the craftsmanship in Zen's bokuto. It was made of a much higher quality of wood than the one she trained with back home in her living room with Aiko.

Zen was focused but was very aware that Oksana was observing him and decided to show off a little. Zen called over one of the body guards who also doubled as his sparring partner now and then. The guard took one of the bokutos from the wall mount and took his position. With a loud cry and a sudden burst of energy from Zen, the two men began to fight. After a few quick blows, the two opponents seemed to be about even, but Zen wanted to make sure Oksana saw a few of what he thought were his better moves before stepping up his skill level and actually going in for the point. At that, he really didn't care about his opponent as much as he was wanting to impress Oksana, so when he won the point, he didn't really bother with pulling his blows when striking down his opponent. As the man dropped to his knee in defeat, he relaxed as he often did in the past as if the match was over but this time he wasn't expecting the extra stern blow across his back.

He quickly gave Zen a look that was meant to say how that was uncalled for but then he realized he was trying to impress the girl. His position was to guard and take care of Zen as per his job requirements that had been handed down to him by Kamiko, so he stayed down even though his instinct was to get to his feet and teach this boy a lesson.

Zen glanced over at Oksana and his ego took the expression on her face as she was not impressed by his fighting skills, when in reality; she was not impressed at how he treated the men who were there for him and were trained to give their lives for him if need be. Zen began to do a series of moves that were part of his exercise routine.

The workout was to show the different skills of each of the animals associated with the skill. Oksana could see his body language was that of a tiger stalking his prey then quickly pouncing. He then moved into a skill that was of a snake that blended into that of a crane that led into a quick strike pose.

Oksana recognized the trend when he went to into a routine that mimicked the motions of the monkey. This seemed to be what he was most accomplished at and Oksana took as his go to skill, his quickness. She thought to herself, this was his way of saving his best skill for last. At the same time, she remembered what Aiko said, "Pursue your skills as one. Do not rely on one over the other and learn them equally, as not to give your opponent an advantage by showing a weakness."

After Zen was done showing off his routine Oksana had a wry smile that seemed to get under Zen's skin.

Zen began to move in a pattern of like a tornado dancing. He whirled slowly at first then began to pick up speed but always maintained control. Oksana sensed the power one could release with a heel kick to the body and saw it coming. Zen had no intention of striking Oksana but when he dug one heel into the mat and threw the other up toward Oksana's face, Zen masterfully stopped his momentum with what he thought might be inches away from her chin. But to his surprise, Oksana anticipated and had taken a couple of steps to the side and was clearly out of reach of what Zen thought could have been an impressive show of his martial arts skills, only to find the two men guarding Oksana trying to hold in a smirk.

Zen didn't need this humiliation from his men and walked over to the guard he had just disrespected and took the bokuto from him and approached Oksana, "You think you can do better?"

Zen handed the bokuto to Oksana who could feel herself gripping the wooden sword tightly as she felt a sense of rage beginning to flow through her. Then she felt the meaning of Aiko's words come through her and she felt a sense of pride as she loosened her grip on the bokuto. The lesson was, "Never let your anger get the best of you and always stay calm, that is your center."

Instead she did the best next thing, so she thought.

As Zen turned and walked back to the center of the dojo, Oksana flipped the wooden sword like a baseball player flipping a bat in the on-deck circle. As soon as she regripped it, with a flick of her wrist, she whipped the bokuto through the air like a helicopter blade toward Zen.

Zen quickly turned and caught the bokuto as if he was expecting it, "Too slow."

CHAPTER 18

Aiko could see ripples of heat waves coming up off of the hot tarmac through the plane's doubled paned windows as the jet was waiting for clearance for takeoff. She tilted her head back and used the stream of cool air from the individual air vent above her to help brush away the loose strand of her hair that had slightly attached itself to her eyelash. As much as Kyle wanted to reach over and help her with her dilemma, Kyle was in the same predicament as her. Kyle and Aiko were both buckled into their seats and handcuffed.

Sakura took a seat across from them, next to Oksana, who was in the seat next to the window. Sakura was holding the katana known as, The Guardian.

Sakura wanted to show Kyle and Aiko her authority and at the same time put a wedge of self-doubt between them and Oksana, "Oksana has been a great help."

Sakura handed the katana to Oksana for two reasons, to show Oksana was not handcuffed herself and to portray the illusion of trust. Oksana wanted to let Kyle and Aiko know that she was not cooperating and minutely shook her head.

Sakura continued with her spiel, "She has been telling me about your little adventure."

Kyle wasn't playing her game, "This adventure is all yours. Oksana has nothing to do with it."

"Sure, she does. You need to get her back to the President before it is too late."

Kyle and Aiko looked at each other, then at Oksana. They had to wonder, had they gotten something out of Oksana, was she bluffing, or did they have somebody already on the inside?

Again, Oksana slowly shook her head.

Kyle believed in Oksana but could not call her bluff without giving her a response that might confirm a probing question so he tried to play it cool, "We brought you the sword. We kept our end of the deal."

"What am I supposed to do, let you go before the family reunion?"

Aiko was firm in her conviction, "I have no family here."

"Of course, you do. You are a Masato."

"That name means nothing to me."

"It should. The family business is running strong here in your homeland."

"I want nothing to do with it. You seem to want it, Sakura. You can have it."

"Oh, Aiko. You truly have no idea."

The plane's steward approached, "The pilot has let me know we have refueled and have clearance. We should be arriving in Niigata in about an hour."

Sakura nodded slightly, "Thank you. Please tell the pilot we will be ready."

The steward headed to the cockpit.

Sakura focused on Kyle and Aiko, "Before we head to Sapporo, we are going to make a stop at one of our factories and check on the distribution of some of our latest inventory."

Neither Kyle or Aiko gave a response, as if it would've mattered.

While Sakura was pushing her little game of mistrust and inquiry, Oksana had been holding the katana in her lap. She had her right hand on the scabbard and rested her left hand over the edge of the hilt.

With the tension being passed back and forth Oksana realized she had been gripping the hilt quite firmly and when she relaxed her hand, she turned it over, and saw the pattern of a few of the letters had been imprinted in her palm. She looked at Kyle who caught a glimpse of the impression as well and tried not to show any reaction but Oksana saw the intense look in his eyes. Oksana quickly turned her hand over as not to let Sakura see the impressions of the ancient text.

Oksana began to slowly rub her palm on the end of the arm rest without trying to draw any attention. It seemed to be working but with lightning reflexes, Sakura grabbed her left wrist and asked, "What do you have in your hand?"

Oksana tried not to show any panic as she tensed her arm slightly, "Nothing."

As Sakura gripped Oksana's wrist, Oksana opened and closed her hand quickly a few times as if to show there was nothing there. Her intensions were to try to get the circulation flowing back into her hand.

Sakura slowly turned over Oksana's hand and revealed that, yes, Oksana had nothing in her hand. What was left of the text had faded to merely a light blush of a mark.

Sakura took the katana back from Oksana, "Okay then."

Kyle nor Aiko noticed that Sakura's little jab was just a distraction while the steward that had walked past her had stopped and was standing next to Kyle.

The steward casually leaned over and with precision, injected Kyle in the arm with a syringe. Within seconds Kyle felt the light sting of the needle turn to a warmth that quickly overcame his senses. As hard as Kyle tried, he could not fight the inevitable, and the warmth turned to a loss of consciousness and he was out.

Aiko tried to maneuver but to no avail. The steward pinned her to the seat with his forearm and then injected her as well.

Oksana could only watch as she saw the person she knew as Aiko lose her natural abilities and saw her body give in to the sedation.

Sakura got in the last word as Aiko fell into the submission of the sedative, "Happy landings."

****

The private jet, call sign MST-1, received word from the Niigata tower that they had been cleared for landing and as it broke through the clouds, the landing gear came down and locked into place. The flaps lowered and the jet's engines rolled back for approach. On touchdown, no one really took notice of the Marine Science Technologies jet as it taxied to the end of the runway, turned, and made its way to the smaller hangers that were at the far end of the airport, away from the larger commercial jets. The sun danced along the plane's chrome accented trim until it took haven in the shade of the awaiting private hanger. Once there, the local crew quickly set wheel chocks in place as soon as the jet came to rest.

A black Mercedes-Benz S-class sedan and a black V-class van had been standing by and as soon as the crew cleared, the two vehicles rolled up near the plane just as the door to the jet was opened and the stairs were deployed.

Sakura was first off followed by Oksana. As soon as Oksana cleared the last step, Sakura quickly led her over to the sedan where the driver had the back door already open and waiting. Oksana tried to stall and take a good look around but Sakura used her momentum to get Oksana quickly into the back of the car. Once they were both inside the driver closed the door.

It was taking Kyle a little longer to get down the stairs as he was a little groggy and he and Aiko were still handcuffed. At one point, he nearly fell but Aiko was just one step below and let Kyle lean on her as needed to steady himself to make it down the last few steps. The doors to the van were already open and the driver and a guard helped Kyle and Aiko into the van and seat belted them in.

Even the luggage was all loaded in the back end of the van and as all the doors seemed to close at once, the air pressure created didn't help Kyle's pounding headache as the lasting effects of the drug were wearing off.

The sedan with Sakura and Oksana cut in front of the van containing Kyle and Aiko and as soon as it cleared, the driver put it in gear and followed. It didn't take long before both cars were already clearing customs and had exited the airport.

Kyle and Aiko were handcuffed in the captain's chairs that made up the second row of seats in the van. It didn't take much of the van not missing a pot hole to shift the luggage and send a small suitcase into the back of Kyle's headrest with a thud.

The thump seemed to bring Kyle to his senses from the effects of the drugs. When he finally got his bearing's, he realized Aiko had been awake a lot longer than him, "Do you have any idea where were going?"

"I'm not sure. They were talking about making a stop before we head on to Sapporo."

"Do you know why? What's there?"

"As I was coming to, I heard Sakura talking to the steward about checking on some new merchandise. Someplace along the coast. A port of some kind that was bringing in a shipment."

"A shipment of what?"

CHAPTER 19

A Japan Lines container ship hauling some two-hundred and fifty containers had slowed to almost a full stop as it was on a tight schedule as it made its way through the Sea of Japan. The freighter was keeping pace with a smaller vessel while it was attempting to unload a large wooden crate that was eight feet square. The forklift operator picked up the crate, moved forward and lowered it onto a cargo net made of rope that had been spread out on the deck of the ship. Workers quickly moved in and brought up the corners of the net as a crane operator swung a large hook over into place. Once all four corners of the net were attached to the hook, one of the workers gave the okay, and the box was raised up. Between the weight of the contents of the crate and the worn cargo net, one corner of the netting was frayed and when the contents shifted in the crate, one of the braids in the rope snapped, putting more tension on the few that were left. The operator swung the crate over the edge of the ship high above the fishing trawler below.

The fishing trawler moved in close and matched speed with the ship. The crate was lowered onto the deck of the fishing boat. The fishermen undid the net, rocked the large crate from one side to the other to get the cargo net freed.

In doing so, as the crate was on one edge, a piece of the netting got caught, so a couple of the men took hold and forcefully worked it free by jerking it out from under the edge of the crate. They hadn't noticed the frayed corner was damaged and working it loose from the crate had made it worse. They placed the net back onto the hook to be returned to the ship.

A second crate of similar size was brought over by the forklift and set down once again onto the cargo net. The corners attached to the hook and the okay was given. The crane operator hit the lever to raise the net and just as he had the crate about to go over the edge of the ship, the weakened corner of the cargo net began to snap. First one piece of the braid and then another. The last piece had been stretched to its limit and then snapped. The crate and its contents shifted and hit the top edge of ship's rail as it was being swung over the edge.

Screams began coming from inside the crate of frightened young women.

Crew members from both ships backed off as the crane operator got control and let the crate bang hard against the edge of the ship to counter its swing.

More screams but this time not as loud as their plea for help was being drowned out from the roar of the ocean as its waves slapped against both sides of the ships.

The crate was already over the edge of the ship so the crane operator quickly lowered the cargo net and its contents down onto the fishing trawler below.

The wooden box and its contents landed on the deck next to the first crate with a hard thud.

Both ships got quickly underway and headed off in opposite directions so as not to lose any more time than needed from their designated route.

Aboard the fishing trawler, the crews went back to work checking their baskets and resetting their traps as usual.

The first mate grabbed a crowbar and began to open one of the crates. He took a moment to wipe the sweat from his brow then continued. He noticed a finger sticking out a small hole from inside the crate and paused long enough to whack it with the crowbar.

He heard a girl's voice from inside the box yelp. The Captain was approaching when he saw the man whack the girl's finger. He took the crowbar from the man and sent him off to do another task then he continued to work on the lid of the wooden crate until he finally got it open and looked inside.

Four girls, all between the ages of 15 and 17 years old, were all under fed and wearing the same soiled clothes they had been in for days. One of the girls was named, Sachi, and had been separated from her older sister, Mai, who was in the other crate.

The Captain opened the second crate to inspect his precious cargo. Another four girls all about the same age. One was dead.

Her neck had been broken when the crate hit the side of the ship. He thought the girls must have tumbled around a bit when the crate went off kilter and she was in an awkward position when the box hit the side of the ship. He wasn't upset that the girl was dead as much as he only got paid if they were alive and able to be cleaned up and in good health. Unfortunately, these two crates were misplaced and the girls had to spend two extra days without food and water.

The Captain called over two crewmen to remove the girl that had died. Young Sachi saw that the lifeless girl they were pulling out of the crate was her sister and began to scream, "Mai! Mai!"

The Captain grabbed Sachi by the throat and squeezed. Sachi was unable to speak and at any moment was about to be unable to breathe. The captain had already had one loss on this trip and thought financially the better of it and let Sachi go. Sachi fell to the floor and could see the emptiness in her sister's eyes as they hauled her on by.

They were about to toss her body overboard when the Captain noticed one of his crew members was reaching into the bin they used to stock the bait for the crab traps. He pulled out a piece of liver from a cow, cut it in half, and toss it to another man who was baiting the traps. He motioned to the two men who were holding the girl's body and pointed to the chopping table. The men did as they were instructed and tossed the girl's deceased body next to the bait well.

The fishing trawler made its way into the Niigata Port through the traffic of other trawlers that were already heading back out to sea.

As far as everyone one else was concerned, it was just another day in the life of this treacherous fishing port but only a few knew that this boat's cargo was hauling something worth more than a regular day's catch.

The crates were offloaded onto a flatbed truck, tied down with straps, then a tarp was added to cover the crates. The tarp made the horrid conditions worse by trapping in the hot air. The few dozen holes that were drilled in the sides of the crates couldn't vent enough fresh air to begin with. The girls had been washed down, given food, and fresh water but that didn't make it any better to breath. One of the girls began to cough and the other girls in the crate put a finger to their lips giving the sign to stay quiet like they were told. The closer they got to the gate, the girl's coughing had gotten worse. Sachi tore away a piece of cloth from the hem of her shirt, poured some of her bottled water over it, then put it to the girl's mouth to use as a filter to stop her from coughing. After a few deep breaths, it seemed to be working.

The flatbed's diesel engine idled as it slowed to a stop to get clearance at the private exit gate.

The guard on duty had been under paid as it was to pretend to scan the manifest and was about to give the all clear when he heard something from under the tarp.

He took a slow walk along the side of the flatbed and when he got to the end, he looked under the tarp. The truck's loud idle and exhaust was quickly getting to him and he was about to lower the tarp when he heard the noise again. A cough.

The guard took a good look and saw the large holes that had been drilled into the sides of a couple of the crates. He thought he saw movement but wasn't sure, that is, until he saw the fear in the eye of a young girl looking back at him through one of the holes. The guard dropped the tarp and as he walked up to the front of the truck, he had placed his hand over the revolver on his hip. When the guard reached the driver's window, he handed the driver back his manifest and just stood there. Without a word, the driver was handed another small envelope from the man in the passenger seat, which in turn he handed to the guard, and the gate was lifted.

The truck's roar from its heavy-duty engine was loud enough as it rumbled along the semi-paved roadway to cover any of the coughing and whimpering that might have escaped from the crates for any passersby to hear.

The girls inside the crates had lost all sense of direction as soon as the truck left the shipyard. Once the noise of the ship's horns and cranes had dissipated, so had their hopes. All they ever had was each other and the likelihood of ever seeing their families again was sinking in.

Sachi thought about just last week playing with her sister down by the water as they splashed each other without a care in the world. Then after, walking with her back home down the street they knew so well.

The truck hit a pothole as it went off the paved road to a dirt side road. The jolt caused all the girls to grab onto each other for safety.

Sachi reached out to take her sister Mai's hand and when she felt one of the other girls grab onto her, she was reminded of the stranger's hand that had taken her and Mai away from their family.

That last walk home was the last time Sachi was allowed to be a little girl.

CHAPTER 20

The flatbed truck that was carrying the two large wooden crates slowed up for the construction going on near a two-lane bridge. As the truck came to a stop, the dust from the dirt road wafted along and swirled in under the tarp. The dust filtered through a few of the air holes in the crates making the thin air inside worse for the girls to breath.

The flagman eventually waved the truck through and the work crew continued in their wake. Just as the truck crossed over the narrow bridge, it down shifted then drove up to a security gate at a slow speed. That was when one of the guards had to get out from behind the only fan in the guard shack and hit a switch that opened the gate and then a second guard waved them through without stopping. Ahead of them was an old factory that from a distance looked like any other run-down processing plant in the area. As the gates closed behind them the guard called in their arrival over his radio.

The flatbed truck drove up to the side door of the factory, on approach and right on que, the doors opened.

What was left of the paint on the factory's interior walls was curled and hanging on by a thread.

The large pieces of sheet metal rattled and a few flakes of paint snapped off like a thin piece of brittle and floated down through beams of sunlight that randomly perforated the walls. Most of the out dated commercial machinery didn't work and was shoved off and stacked into the corner.

This location was just one of the random fronts for temporary layovers for the import and export of human trafficking. The truck came to a full stop and handlers quickly released the straps, removed the tarp, and unloaded the two crates holding the remaining seven girls. Several men stood by as a couple of them opened the wooden boxes. As they helped the girls out one by one, the other men each took a girl and led them over to a makeshift holding cell. One at a time the girls had their clothes removed and were hosed down with a makeshift fire hose. There were a couple of women who gathered up the old clothes and tossed them into a fifty-five-gallon drum that had a fire going to burn the clothes and get rid of the lice and any other contaminations.

A woman was going through a barrel of various styles and sizes of clothing randomly tossing what she thought might fit the girl closest to her at the time.

Without even having a chance to dry off, the girls were quickly getting dressed and grabbing whatever clothes they could get before they were passed on to the next stage. Sachi grabbed up a few pieces of extra clothing and tucked them under her shirt. If their hair was longer than shoulder length, it was immediately cut to that standard.

Like the next stage in a factory line, each girl was given a pair of cheap flip-flops and passed on down the line. One of the girls slowed the line from moving when she suddenly stopped after hearing a loud roar from a crowd of men gathered in a circle. It really wasn't the roar as much as what she thought she saw, what they were all cheering about.

She saw a rope hanging down from a ceiling joint that disappeared into the center of the crowd, then for a moment, there was a small gap in the crowd and in that moment, she thought she saw a man at the end of that rope, yet he seemed to be floating.

The crowd had formed a large circle, three deep. As the dust settled from most of the crowd trying to jockey for position, they were waiting to see how long the barefoot man who stood on the eighteen-inch-high bamboo poles could go without falling off. The bamboo poles were only four inches around and stood on end.

The man's legs were beginning to shake. He could feel the rough edges where the bamboo was cut and the splintered edges were digging into the soles of his feet as he was beginning to lose his stamina and balance. It was only eighteen-inches high and not a very big fall, except for the noose that was around his neck.

His body was covered in sweat and the fray from the rope was rubbing his skin raw.

The salt from his sweat was seeping into his open irritated skin was not his worry, how much longer could he hold out without hanging himself was the foremost thing on his mind.

A few of the men in the crowd had started quietly making wagers. Then from somewhere beyond the crowd, someone had thrown an empty glass coke bottle, hitting the man in the noose in the head. He almost fell off the bamboo and the ones making wagers in the crowd starting yelling as it seemed someone was trying to hedge their bets.

The man had his head down trying to shake off the blow to the head and quickly gained back his senses, then looked up at the men as if to say, I'm still here. The man trying to hold out from hanging himself was Kyle.

The woman in the white gloves was in her office inspecting the detail and craftmanship of the Guardian katana. The sounds of the crowd were gaining in enthusiasm. From the factory floor, she could hear a faint crack of a whip and the crowd roared even louder. She set the katana down on a large black velvet pad. Her focus was now on the spectacle that was now taking place on the floor of her factory.

The back of Kyle's shirt had two tears in it from the end of the whip having torn through it like it was tissue. Blood and sweat exploding from the torn flesh along with Kyle's involuntarily body flinches and screams were unlike any other.

His legs were wobbling from trying to hold off from cramping. The bamboo poles he was balancing on started to rock then settle as Kyle got his control back as not to fall off.

Off to one side of the crowd, a guard dressed in fatigues was holding onto Aiko's left arm. With Aiko's right arm, she was holding Oksana tight against her and trying to shelter Oksana's view so she could not see what was happening to Kyle.

The man with the whip approached Aiko, "Tell us what you know about the swords and the secret they hold regarding the location of the Monarch Moon and this will all end."

"I told you, we don't know."

The man walked back to the center of the circle and took his position behind Kyle. He stroked his whip and got a measure for the distance then he let it crack.
Upon contact, Kyle's whole body flinched so hard he lost his footing on one of the poles. He was now only standing with all of his weight on one of the poles.

Two Guards that were supposed to be watching the exits had instead been making wagers on the life and death outcome of Kyle's balancing act. They exchanged money after one of them lost to the other over Kyle being able to hold on, even if only standing on a single bamboo post. The guard held up two fingers to gesture if the other man would like to double down. The second man had lost what he had so he offered up a cell phone. Kyle's cell phone.

The man with the whip whirled, and crack! The tip of the whip struck right on the back of Kyle's thigh of the leg he was standing on. His leg buckled a bit and Kyle was straining with his neck in the rope as a counterbalance to his free leg as he tried not to fall.

Kyle's focus was so intent on staying alive, trying not to think about the pain, that all of his senses were heightened. Even in all of the chaos, Kyle caught a glimpse of his cell phone being passed from one guard to another as the winning guard collected his bet and put it in his shirt pocket.

The man with the whip looked at Aiko, and shrugged. Aiko's eyes were filled with tears. She was silent. The man swirled the whip and laid out its full length and wrapped the end of the whip around the bamboo pole Kyle was balancing on and was about to pull it out from under him when he made one more look back at Aiko. The man yanked on the whip and pulled out the bamboo pole.

Just as Kyle dropped, Aiko broke free from her captor leaving Oksana behind and ran to Kyle. She put herself between Kyle's legs and lifted Kyle up onto her shoulders.

Kyle got his concentration back as he realized he was not dangling from the end of the rope. There was still tension as he must still help Aiko to keep his balance as he sat on her shoulders.

The crowd was in amazement as no one saw this coming. The crowd cheered in unison then they went silent as the man with the whip cracked one off in the air.

Oksana wanted to go help Aiko but the man was holding her back. Kyle knew they wanted blood and there had to be a sacrifice, "Aiko. Don't."

Kyle heard another crack of the whip and yet he did not feel it. What Kyle could feel was Aiko's legs weaken as the shock of the whip to Aiko's back made her body jolt in pain. Aiko's shirt was partially torn and no one had noticed her tattoo yet.

Oksana screamed out in terror, "Aiko!"

The whip whirled around again, crack! This time Aiko's shirt ripped open even wider. The strain Aiko was under was immense but she held strong.

The whip began to circle about to make another pass and was on the back swing when a woman's silhouette appeared in the shadow behind the man with the whip.

The woman with the white gloves showed her precision as she drew the Guardian from its scabbard in one shimmering movement. With a flick of her wrist, as the whip circled back before being thrust forward, she cut away two feet from the end of the braided leather whip.

The man whirling the whip felt his effort fail and come up short as the forward motion did not reach its intended target.

He turned back and saw Kamiko Masato walk past him and up to Kyle as she raised the Guardian once more and cut the rope above Kyle's head. Both Kyle and Aiko fell to the ground.

Oksana's guard relaxed his grip and Oksana pulled away, grabbed a boat oar off a nearby shelf, and cracked it across the guard's shin. The guard screamed as he bent over and grabbed his leg.

That was when Oksana swung the oar back up and cracked the guard across the forehead knocking him off his feet. Oksana ran to the aide of Kyle and Aiko. Oksana stood at the ready holding up the oar like a bokuto willing to take on anyone who tried to approach as Kyle and Aiko made sure they were each alright.

From out of the shadows, Kamiko Masato, stepped forward and using her white gloved hands, slipped the Guardian back into its scabbard. Kamiko was a beautiful woman in her mid-forties, very fit, and very confident. Everything she did had no wasted movement to it right down to the way she walked to within a few feet of Oksana.

"Hello Oksana. My name is Kamiko Masato."

Oksana was still clutching the oar and ready to use it.

Kamiko tried to put Oksana at ease, "There is no need for that oar."

Kyle and Aiko stood. Aiko took the oar from Oksana and dropped it on the ground.

Kamiko took a step forward, "I'm sorry we had to meet this way and under these circumstances. My assistant will help you clean up and look after your needs. When you are ready, we will talk." Kamiko turned and walked away.

Kyle could see the look in Aiko's face that was one of disgrace and anger. He could see Aiko wanted no part of this. Kyle put one arm around Aiko and with his other hand raised her chin so he could look into her eyes.

He could see she felt ashamed but that was not what he felt at all, "You saved my life. You are amazing and what you did took great courage."

Sakura came forward with a couple of henchmen, "Come with me. I think you'll find this interesting."

CHAPTER 21

Sakura entered the large open room where all the research and artifacts covered the elongated tables. She was followed by Kyle, Aiko, and Oksana. The henchmen stayed back at the doorway.

Sakura pointed out a bowl of fruit on the end of one of the tables.

"May I offer you something to eat?"

"No thank you," Oksana said as she walked off in a trance right over to the human pelt of the yakuza. Oksana picked up the piece that was taken from them, the legend, and showed it to Aiko.

Kyle and Aiko watched as Kamiko walked over and removed a scarf that was covering a set of swords. Aiko knew right away that it was the same tanto that Oksana had used to kill her father.

On the rung below the tanto was the matching wakizashi. Kamiko had a cloth in her hand and added the finishing touches to wiping down the Guardian, then she raised it, and added it to the third rung below the wakizashi on the display stand. The set was complete.

Oksana was still engrossed in the yakuza tattoo that covered the human pelt. She looked to the side and saw Kamiko's notes and began scanning over them.

It didn't take her long to figure it out, "They're after the Monarch Moon."

Kamiko turned and gave Oksana a stern look. Oksana backed up closer to Kyle as Aiko walked closer to the set of swords.

Aiko tried to take a closer look at the edges of the hilts of all three swords without being too obvious. She noticed they all had the same form of ancient text.

Standing next to Kamiko, Aiko could feel the tension in her body that she had to control, "So, all of this, has been about the swords."

"Not just any swords," Kamiko replied. "These are very special."

Kyle could sense Aiko was not willing to ask, but he was, "Worth killing for?"

Kamiko's response was cold and calculated, "Yes." As Kamiko continued, Kyle wanted nothing more than to walk up and hold Aiko but knew he would be taking away what power and control she had left, "My brother was careless and didn't know their true value. He didn't believe in the legend as I do. He only believed in what he could have right now, and did not look to the future. It cost him everything, including his honor."

Kyle could not hold back his feelings, "Where's the honor in what he did to his own daughter?"

Kamiko hesitated for a moment and looked at Aiko, "Like I said, he was without bushido."

"What is bushido?" Oksana asked.

Kamiko's tone was more defined and had a mysterious element to it, "Aiko is bushido." Kamiko focused her attention on Oksana, "It is an unwritten code of moral principles of the samurai."

Kyle was trying to get a read off of Kamiko, "You have the swords, now what?"

"Now we are one step closer to locating the AMADA, her secrets, and the Monarch Moon."

Kyle was still looking for answers and at the same time was trying not to let Kamiko know just how much they really knew, "What exactly is the Monarch Moon?"

Kamiko turned to another page in the ledger and revealed a sketch of a round gem with a stick figure drawn in the center of it that looked like a butterfly, "This is the original drawing that was made by one of the Japanese fishermen as described to him by the sole survivor of the AMADA. When he was rescued by the fishermen, he told them his ship had been cursed by the Monarch Moon. The man went on to say, the AMADA was out of Spain travelling along the silk route buying and trading when the ship caught fire and went down."

Kamiko opened up another ledger and produced a manifest. "This document shows the AMADA leaving Barcelona Spain and then was reported lost at sea, but not before stopping off in Sri Lanka."

"This is where they got the Monarch Moon?" Kyle probed.

"This is where they, among other priceless gems, acquired a large yellow Sapphire known as the, Luna de Monarca."

Without hesitating Oksana replied, "That is Spanish for Monarch Moon."

Aiko needed to downplay the information, "It's just a legend. A story we were told as children in the orphanage to tell around the campfire."

Sakura confirmed the stories but felt she knew something more, "A legend, yes, because the only man to have seen it, died, but not before the fisherman left a marker. It turns out, it's more than just a story."

Sakura opened a wooden box on the other side of the frame that held the human pelt and removed a piece of scroll that had burn marks around its edges.

Before Sakura could explain, Kamiko took over, "This partial blueprint was discovered after the swordsmith was commissioned to make the swords. He died shortly after and as far as anyone knows, this set of swords was the last he ever made. What is left of the text was a single line and only a few characters of another."

Kyle's investigative mind had to ask, "So, you're saying, why would anyone go to all these lengths if it wasn't true? Still doesn't make it real."

"You tell me, Mr. Morrell. Why would anyone make a one of a kind set of swords that on their own are a treasure, if not to tell us what they are protecting is not legendary?"

As much as Kyle wanted to play it off, curiosity was getting the best of him, "Why hasn't anyone found it by now? The Monarch Moon, that is."

"As you can see, what I have on these tables is years of research and items that have been handed down and entrusted to our family for years. We have proven the legend to be real but all we needed was the correct place to begin our search."

Aiko looked at Kyle and was trying to let him know his questions were leading down a dark path.

"What makes you think we know the location?" asked Aiko.

The sound of Victor Pankov's voice cut through the air like a dagger hitting its mark, "Because I have seen this writing before."

As Pankov walked into the room, Oksana hid behind Kyle using him as a shield.

Pankov walked up to Aiko, "You don't look surprised to see me."

"When I saw the tanto you stole from us was here, I figured it was you Kamiko was referring to when she said, "We have proven the legend to be true."

"So here is what is going to happen next. Either you tell us what you know about the location or Oksana goes back on the block to the highest bidder."

Kyle felt Oksana being pulled away from him from behind as he turned to see a guard forcing her toward the exit.

As he tried to reach out for her, another guard grabbed him from behind, turned his head to one side, and put a knife to his throat.

Oksana started to scream and the guard already had a rag doused in chloroform ready.

Aiko caught Pankov's attention, "Stop!" Pankov raised his hand and the guard stop.

Aiko knew she had to give them something, "I'll tell you."

Pankov had been waiting for this moment, "Yes, you will." Pankov moved closer to the human pelt as if it held the answer, "Show us."

Aiko reached up and grabbed the Guardian from the display stand.

One of Pankov's guards drew his gun and aimed it at Aiko.

Kyle flinched as he tried to speak. That was enough for the knife, that was pressed against his throat, to cut him slightly, "Wait…"

Kamiko held up her palm to Pankov and everyone froze.

Aiko used what leverage she had left, "Tell the guard to back away."

Kamiko nodded to the guard who took his knife away from Kyle's throat. Before he took a step back, the guard wiped the blood from the edge of the knife onto Kyle's shoulder.

Aiko turned to a blank page in Kamiko's journal then moved over closer to Kyle.

She took her thumb and rubbed off some of the blood from Kyle's throat then rubbed Kyle's blood from her thumb over the outside edge of the Guardian's hilt.
Kyle and Aiko shared a look of deep concern and love for one another.

Aiko turned and rolled out the text from the side of the hilt onto the blank page and the ancient text appeared in blood.

****

The photograph President Dalton held was a copy from the crime scene at Kyle's beach house of the blood-stained floor. Dalton laid the photograph on the coffee table in the Oval Office that divided the two couches in the main sitting area, "Are you sure about this?"

Wintersteen closed the file he was holding, "Yes. The blood at the scene is a match to one of the men that was killed and the writing has been verified. It says, Sado Shima."

CHAPTER 22

Kamiko took a moment to look around her own collection of art and memorabilia on the walls of her personal museum. In her head, she had a number that was close to the value, but the most priceless work of art right now were the last three swords ever commissioned by the master swordsmith, Masamune.

All three edges of the hilts had been stained and the text on each of the swords had been revealed. Three lines, side by side, that ran vertically from top to bottom as Japanese text was meant to be read.

Aiko and Kamiko took a closer look.

Aiko had to find out just how much Kamiko already knew, "This is very old text."

"It's called, Kojiki."

Kyle looked over Aiko's shoulder, "Can you read it? What does it say?"

Aiko studied the text over and over, "I'm not really sure."

Kamiko knew the text, "It tells of a legend, a treasure, and a location."

Pankov was focused on the end result, "The Monarch Moon."

Kamiko confirmed, "Yes."

Pankov came in closer to see the text up close for himself, "Can you translate it? Does it tell us anything about its weight or true value?"

When the text was rolled onto the paper from the tanto, it was hard to tell where the sentence began and where it ended. Kamiko drew a line where she believed the text began and where it started to repeat.

She then drew a line through the words on each end canceling out where they repeated, just leaving the necessary text and read what was left, "The first line says, The Monarch Moon is marked by death."

Kyle remembered, "Sakura mentioned the fishermen left a marker."

Kamiko went through the same process and found where the second sentence from the wakizashi began, "The second line reads, The Takara Uso No ma ni"

Aiko translated, "The treasure lies between."

Pankov asked, "Between what?"

Kamiko ran her finger down the last line of the text from the katana's hilt, "That is in the third line. Niigata Sado Shina." Kamiko point to a map showing their location in Niigata, "Between here and the island of Sado."

Kyle felt he needed to interject some self-doubt, "How do you even know the legend is true or if there was such a ship, let alone a precious stone worth all of this?"

Kamiko began to pace along the long edge of the table and looked at all the research and clues she had collected over the years, "Mr. Morrell, let me tell you a story."

Kamiko grabbed a handful of documentation in each hand, "All of this is real." Kamiko then dropped the papers on the table like leaves falling under the tree, presenting them as something tangible. "Our family has been in this area long before the AMADA went down and were fishermen working these waters that very day. This story has been passed down from generation to generation. It was my ancestors who were there to rescue the sole survivor, a pirate, who told them about the treasure the AMADA carried."

Oksana envisioned a chest full of gold, "There was more than the Monarch Moon?"

Kamiko played into her fantasy, "Yes, a lot more. So much so, they had to leave a marker so over the years they could come back and plunder it, and they did."

Oksana was feeling the fever, "What kind of marker?"

"The pirate himself. First, they tied his hands and feet, then they attached a ballast stone to hold him in place on the reef below." Kamiko raised one finger for effect, "But, not before begging for his life, telling them about a stone so magnificent it was referred to as, the Monarch Moon."

Oksana imagined holding the precious gem in her hand and looking at it, "Why is it called, the Monarch Moon?"

Kamiko knew she had an audience, "The pirate was telling them anything he could to convince them to spare his life. So, he spun this tale of a perfectly round cut yellow Sapphire that when light passes through it, it projects what appears to be the shape of a monarch butterfly."

Oksana was like a kid in a candy store, "So, why did they use the pirate as the marker?"

"When they asked him to produce the Sapphire and he could not, they knew they could not let him live and risk the story getting out."

Again, Kyle tried to poke holes in the story, "What's to say any of this is true? What if this is just a bedtime story passed down to help you sleep at night?"

Kamiko's pacing had led her to the end of one of the tables full of artifacts. On the end was a silk scarf covering a discernible object. Kamiko pulled off the scarf.

There, on the end of the table, was the ship's bell from the AMADA.

****

The Spanish galleon, the AMADA, was docked at the coastal city of Mombasa, which today is Kenya's second largest city next to the capitol, Nairobi. The first mate reached out and rang the ship's pristine brass bell three times.

The ship's crew was about to withdraw the boarding plank from the dock when a last crew member jumped onto the plank, quick stepped his way across onto the ship, then two men pulled up the plank and stowed it away. Half of the ship's crew was new so the men had no reason to suspect the man they just let aboard was not one of their own. This stowaway went by the name of Federico Vargas. His friends used to refer to him as, five finger Freddy. That is, until he had no friends. He and his mates had once tried to start a mutiny that also involved kidnapping the Captain's daughter. When the attempt failed, Vargas was the only survivor to be set adrift, leaving his fate to the sea.

As fate would have it, Vargas knew he was living on borrowed time, because what fate hadn't accounted for was Vargas didn't care if he lived or died. He was a child born at sea to a mother who had no name. She had been purchased along with the other goods before getting underway on the AMADA'S maiden voyage. As long as Vargas could remember, he had been working long, hard days at any port that would take him along the silk route shipping lanes, hoping one day to have enough money and respect to captain his own ship.

One day, a man on his death bed, who had worked along-side him on a ship called the SCAVANGER, claimed to be his father. Ever since that day, he held onto another man's memories of his only knowledge of his mother to drive him to one day find the AMADA.

This was that day. Vargas had just returned from a six-month voyage and had taken a few days off to get drunk, have a good woman, and sleep. After spending more money than he should have, and more days on land than he had in a very long time, he decided to go down and take a look at this Spanish galleon he had heard about that had docked for supplies a few days earlier. The closer he got to the ship he couldn't believe his eyes. It was, the AMADA.

When he heard her bell ring three times he didn't hesitate. Vargas was going to make that ship one way or another. Instinct told him that there had to be new faces on board so why couldn't he be one of them? When he saw her boarding plank about to be withdrawn, he boarded. He felt this was his destiny and if he worked hard no one would notice until it was too late. As he boarded he saw the ship's captain being handed a map. Vargas didn't care where the AMADA was headed as long as he was aboard.

The Spanish galleon's captain rolled out a map showing the latest ports of call for trading at the time, that being 1807. The previous map was based on Venetian explorer, Marco Polo, who was one of the first Europeans to use the intended course known as, the Silk Routes.

These ships were known as a Manila Galleon or the New Spain, also known as, La Nao de la China, meaning the China Ship.

The Spanish mainly used them to sail the trade routes from Manila to the Philippines from 1565 to 1815 carrying Chinese goods.

These Manila galleons were used to bring Spain their cargoes of marketable goods and up until 1815, when the Mexican War of Independence ended the Spanish occupying the ports of Mexico.

The captain traced his finger along his planned route taking he and his crew from Mombasa up North to a couple of stops in Arabia. After that, across the Arabia Sea to the city of Quilon near the southern tip of India. After restocking the ship, the AMADA was on to Sri Lanka.

Vargas had been to Sri Lanka before. His previous visit was to see if he could find anyone who knew his mother. The dying man had said she was the daughter of a wealthy man from Sri Lanka who had abandoned his daughter after she gotten involved with a young man from her village. This was not in her father's plans as she had been promised to the son of a local business man her father was indebted to. This was his chance to make the rounds again and see if he could validate the old man's memories. Or, was it just a story?

Vargas had very little time before the AMADA was to get under way so he stayed close to the docks and stopped by a few of the local businesses trying to get any information that could lead him to finding his mother's family.

After checking out a few shops with no luck, he decided to try the exchange where businessmen made deals for land, goods, and other needs that needed lots of cash.

Just as he entered the exchange, he was immediately asked to leave and he did, but not before seeing a man closing up a small leather satchel of gems. That man was the captain of the AMADA.

While Vargas waited outside the modest import export business, he saw a couple of transients eyeing the door to the exchange. After twenty minutes, the men were still there and then he saw his captain emerge from the exchange surrounded by two guards.

He had intended to point out the wary strangers to his captain but as he was about to walk up to him, he glanced over and noticed the two men were no longer there.

Vargas figured the captain was safe and he knew the ship would be sailing soon so he took what little time he had left to try a few more local businesses. He was looking for some sort of closure, not knowing when the next time or if ever he would be docking in Sri Lanka again.

Once back aboard the AMADA and the ship was underway through the Bay of Bengal on route to Calcutta, Vargas kept his head down and his eyes and ears open for any scuttlebutt aboard ship about the precious gems.

A week had gone by and no one had mentioned a thing. This had brought Vargas to the conclusion that this was no ordinary voyage. He knew there were ships out there that covered as cargo ships that from time to time would carry something so precious only the captain knew of its true value and destination.

If these gems had gone through the normal channels and the word got out, the ship would be in jeopardy of being overrun by pirates.

Vargas had been at sea on the AMADA for a couple of weeks and seemed to be as much a part of the crew as the next man so when he saw the captain alone he took a moment to ask, "Excuse me, Captain Rivera. May I have a moment of your time?"

"Yes, what is it?"

"Sir, my name is Vargas, Federico Vargas."

"Is that name supposed to mean something to me?"

"Well sir, maybe not, but I was wondering about another name. Daniella Machado. She was of Portuguese decent. Her father was a merchant of the isle of Sri Lanka."

Captain Rivera thought about it for a minute, "Yeah, I knew a merchant by that name. I heard he killed himself after he found his daughter had taken her own life on a sailing ship. This ship."

"Is it true?"

"Why do you want to know?"

"If what I was told is true, she was my mother."

Before the captain could reply a shout came from high above from the lookout in the crow's nest followed by the sound of men urgently scurrying about the ship.

"Ship on the horizon!"

The first mate replied, "Is it flying any colors?"

The man in the crow's nest took a look through his leather-bound telescope and what he saw made him fear the worst, the ship heading their way was flying the Jolly Roger.

"Pirates!"

It crossed Vargas' mind that it must have been the two men outside the merchant's exchange, pirates.
The captain grabbed his first mate and Vargas and said, "You two, come with me."

Inside the captain's quarters, the captain pulled up a trap door in the corner of the floor and ordered both Vargas and the first mate to gather all documents that were out on the table and to put them in the hidden compartment. As they did, Vargas saw a small powder keg and a musket pistol in the hold. The two men quickly shoved all the maps and documents they could down and around the keg.

Vargas kept an eye on the captain and saw him hide away a few smaller private things in another hidden compartment behind the shelving beyond his desk.

Vargas had the sense that the captain knew his ship, the AMADA, was not going to outrun the pirate ship and had to make his galleon look like any other cargo hauler in the silk route shipping lanes.

The pirate ship, the MIDNIGHT STAR, finally did overtake the AMADA and her crew without firing a single cannon. It wasn't long before Captain Rivera and his lieutenants were set adrift in a row boat and left to fend for themselves.

They were given a small ration of food and water and left to be found by the next ship that happened to sail by. These ships didn't have regular intervals and it was just a matter of luck that two days later they were rescued, but not before the pirates had put a lot of distance between the captain and his ship.

Vargas and the remaining crew were now sailing under new orders of Captain Henry Hawkins and according to Hawkins, all remaining crew members were now pirates. If they didn't like the arrangement, they could leave at any time, as chum for the sharks that follow the ships looking for anything they threw over as garbage.

CHAPTER 23

At sea, it is hard enough to keep track of the days but Vargas had begun to lose all sense of time as he and the remaining crew of the AMADA were made to work until they dropped. For some of the men who dropped that was the end, they had given up, and would rather die. They were accommodated.

The word on the ship was the pirates were still looking for a precious one of a kind gem known as Luna de Monarca. It was rumored to have been commissioned by the King of Spain himself, Ferdinand VII, for his second wife to be, his niece, Maria Isabel of Portugal.

One day Vargas was assigned to clean the floors of the captain's quarters. This was his chance. He blocked the door with his mop and quickly checked the hidden compartments. It seemed they had found the documents in the floor boards but not the space behind the desk wall. Vargas opened the pouch and poured out its contents. There in the middle table was the Monarch Moon.

Vargas had to leave the yellow sapphire in its hiding place until they were closer to land. In the mean, time he would do all that he could to stay alive.

Vargas did get a sense from the crew that the AMADA had passed through the South China Sea and was heading Northeast.

The weather was getting worse. The storms were more frequent and the days were getting shorter. Each night they would get their bearings from the stars but the days started with a heavy morning fog and a dark sky with no sun to navigate on the horizon. Not only was there a man in the crow's nest, there were two more men on either side of the ship halfway up the cargo nets that were attached to the mast as secondary lookouts.

Even the ship's figurehead, a piece of Spanish art of a life-size mermaid made from pure mahogany that held out a lantern in front of her to help guide the way. She wore a red, white, and gold breastplate that proudly proclaimed the coat of arms of España.

The fog was so thick, the crew on deck could barely see the men on the sides and only knew the location of the crow's nest from the lookout's lantern illuminating a faint yellow glow.

Then the word came, "Ship, dead ahead!"

The watchman rang the ship's bell sounding the alarm.

The large, looming shadow of darkness turned out not to be a ship but a massive iceberg about the same size and mass as the AMADA.

A second voice desperately called out, "Iceberg! Hard, right full rudder!" Again, the ship's bell rang out but this time it seemed to have a greater sense of urgency.

The captain cranked the ship's wheel hard to the right as fast as he could, sending all eight wooden spokes around like a fan blade centered on its brass hub. Once the wheel came to a full stop hard right, it took a moment for the ship to respond, but she did. As the fog dissipated, everyone on board watched as the iceberg passed by the ship's stern within fifty feet and they all took a sigh of relief.

The watchman turned his gaze back towards the bow and could not get the words out in time, he just began ringing the bell franticly. The crew turned back around and saw that a second iceberg, twice the size of the first, was right in their path and they had no time to turn the ship.

The line to the bell was ripped from the watchman's hand as he was tossed aside from the collision with the frozen monolith.

The first casualty was the ship's figurehead. The wooden mermaid was torn away from the front of the ship like a defenseless piñata. The hull was breached and the ship started taking on water, and fast.

The man in the crow's nest was flung from his post due to the sudden ramming of the iceberg. He hit the deck hard and was killed instantly, followed by his lantern. The lantern smashed into pieces and started a fire on deck. One crewmen tried to put out the fire but the fuel was made from whale oil and was making it very difficult.

A second crewman was there with a small wooden barrel filled with sand for such occasions. The problem quickly became clear, they weren't going to have enough sand.

This wasn't the only lantern to break away. There were now fires breaking out all over the ship. Men began to scramble what few life boats they had left.

Vargas saw the captain helping his men who still had a chance to survive get to the boats. Vargas had one thing on his mind, get to the captain's quarters, and retrieve the Monarch Moon.

When Vargas entered the quarters, it was already a foot deep in water and rising. The collision had busted out a few boards along the port side of the captain's quarters. It was taking Vargas too much time to get to the hidden compartment. The water had shifted most of the wooden furniture up against the bookshelf. Vargas could feel the ship start to list and he used this to his advantage to move the furniture to the side and open the hidden panel.

Vargas grabbed the pouch, opened it, and removed the largest of the precious stones, the Monarch Moon. He tied a knot in the bottom of his shirt using the shirt tails. He added the stone along with a small handful of diamonds he could use as currency. He then tied another knot to hide his plundered booty in a hidden and secure place.

Vargas didn't have much time and headed toward the door.

What he hadn't counted on was when the furniture shifted away from the shelf, it was now stacked up against the door, blocking him in. To make things worse, he could see flames on the other side of the door licking their way in through wherever they could find a gap in the door to the cabin.

Vargas turned and saw the water was still pouring in from the breach and filling the room quickly. Vargas waded waist deep over to the breach. He grabbed one of the loose boards and pulled on it. The board resisted. Vargas was startled when the trap door from the hidden floor compartment surfaced followed by the powder keg. He grabbed the keg, wrapped it in a blanket, and shoved the ends of the blanket into the lose boards of the breach to hold it in place. He punched open the top of the keg with is fist, took the bandana from around his neck, and placed one end of it into the powder keg as a fuse. Vargas then ripped away a piece of dry lumber from the top of the shelf, held one end of it to the fire that was now working its way through the cabin door, and lit the free end of the bandana.

Vargas dove under the water and swam to the starboard side of the cabin. The powder keg blew a large hole in the side of the cabin allowing the room to immediately fill with water.

Topside, every man was for himself. What the flames didn't burn the iceberg had torn apart. The AMADA was going down.

The only survivor seemed to be the ship's figurehead. She had been battle tested and had the scars to prove it. The deity was afloat about thirty feet off the stern when suddenly, Vargas came up from under the water gasping for air. He grabbed onto the carved maiden as if his life depended on it, and it did.

Vargas watched the AMADA as it went up in flames. The ship's bell gave one last clang as it broke away from its post and fell into the sea.

Vargas began to paddle further away from the ship and watched as what was left of her listed and sizzled out. Black smoke and flames danced wildly as one as the AMADA was torn apart. The boards exploded from the heat meeting the icy waters. With one last fiery breath she was extinguished and was engulfed by the sea.

Vargas wasn't the only one watching. Off in the distance, a boat of Japanese fishermen saw the flames, and were already on the way.

By the time the small Japanese fishing boat arrived, the cold waters of the open sea had taken their toll on Vargas, and he was losing his grip on the ship's wooden figurehead. The fishermen quickly helped Vargas into their small boat. They did their best to help the survivor get warm by offering him a blanket. Vargas did not understand the Mandarin language but could tell by their gestures they were suggesting he take off his wet clothes.

This made sense, but Vargas knew he could not risk letting the men know about the precious stones.

Vargas took the blanket and wrapped it around his shoulders covering his upper torso. The night air had a slight breeze that accentuated the chill factor causing Vargas to shake uncontrollably. He tried his best to warm his hands by blowing in them before he attempted to undo the knot on his shirt. Doing his best to hide the stones, he slowly undid the first knot.

A few of the diamonds slipped out of his grasp but he was able to catch them out of mid-air, that is, all but one. It passed through his fingers and onto the deck of the boat. The fishermen began to talk among themselves and Vargas got the sense it was not in his favor. Vargas quickly turned his back to the fishermen, pulled the Monarch Moon from its hiding place, and swallowed it.

Vargas knew he had to face his rescuers and hoped the diamonds would be enough. He turned around and extended his hand offering the fishermen two diamonds. Again, the fishermen talked among themselves before gesturing to Vargas they wanted more. Vargas knew his life was on the line and offered up the rest of the diamonds. Still the fishermen wanted more. Vargas did his best to tell his rescuers that was all he had and threw both hands back in the direction of where the ship went down trying to indicate there could possibly be more on the ship.

The fishermen knew the area well enough to head over where the ship went down to see if it could have possibly come to rest on the coral shelf below.

159

Once they made their way to the floating debris field, one of the fishermen tied a ballast stone to a long rope and dropped it overboard.

Before coming to the end of the rope, the stone reached the bottom letting them know that, yes, they were above the shallow shelf. They retrieved the ballast stone and estimated the depth to be about fifty feet.

Then came the question, "How do we mark the location and keep it a secret?"

One of the fishermen had an answer, he picked up an oar and began beating Vargas with it. A second fishermen grabbed his oar and did the same. Vargas was beaten within an inch of his life. That's when the fishermen tied the ballast stone to his foot and together they tossed Vargas, their marker, overboard.

Vargas' body sank rapidly and his last breath was taken from him when his body lodged itself into the jagged coral shelf that waited below.

CHAPTER 24

President Dalton was holding a small replica of the Liberty Bell. It was a gift from his wife when he decided to run for office as a reminder to always fight for the rights of all Americans, and to uphold not only the constitution, but what its intentions meant then and what they stand for today.

Dalton remembered when he first met his wife in college. She was giving a speech on human rights and she was so passionate about it, he couldn't take his eyes off of her. He saw a fire in her that sparked his interest in politics. He would consistently find himself showing up at any rally she was attending.

One day he was talking to a friend at one of the rallies when a clipboard with a few pieces of line ruled paper was pressed into his hands and a woman's voice said, "Sign this."

He looked up to see the woman that was on the stage a few minutes ago was now right in front of him. Jillian Wilder was even more beautiful up close and the scent of her perfume was intoxicating. Her confidence took his breath away.

Dalton regained his composure, "What am I signing?"

"I'm gathering ten-thousand signatures to send to the United Nations to help generate interest in a declaration of human rights as it pertains to human trafficking."

Dalton didn't bother reading the text at the top of the page. Her voice alone would have had him signing whatever she handed to him.

Dalton finished signing and started to hand her back the clipboard, "How many signatures do you have?"

Jillian pressed it back in his direction, "…and your address.

Just as Dalton was completing his address she added, "Phone number, too." Jillian took a glance at his name, "Spencer."

Spencer did as she requested, "So?"

"So, what?"

"How many signatures do you have…Jillian?"

She liked he already knew her name, "Including yours?" She started to turn and walk away, "One."

Dalton felt a bit of pride as he was the first to help her fulfill her quest. He didn't want her to leave, "It looks like you're going to need some help gathering that many signatures. Can I help?"

Jillian stopped and looked back at him, "Do you really want to spend all your free time walking with me all over this campus and the surrounding neighborhoods to gather signatures?"

Dalton replied, "Don't forget addresses and phone numbers."

"Don't need those. All we need is their signatures."

Jillian turned and walked away and that's when it sank in, she had used these pretenses to get his number.

Dalton felt a rush and a quickness in his step as he caught up to her and has been by her side ever sinse.

Dalton set the paperweight down on the corner of his desk and joined the other two men in the Oval Office who were sitting across from him.

President Dalton looked at the head of the FBI and then at one of his staffers waiting for answer.

The staffer had been working from an iPad feverishly trying to pull up the correct file of information, "Sir, here is the location of the island of Sado. It is just off the Eastern coast of Japan near the city of Niigata."

"What's Niigata known for?" Dalton asked.

"It's a port town, Sir. Shipping and industry mainly."

Wintersteen thought about the benefits of such a location, "It would make it easy to have access for the import and export business of human trafficking."

Dalton did not want to get ahead of himself, he needed to know, "Do the Masato's have any holdings in the area?"

Before the staffer could answer, there was a ping from his tablet. Then another.

"Sir, you wanted to have me tell you if any other dots appeared on the tracking app. Two more just came online."

"Their location?"

"Niigata, Sir."

His reply was followed by another ping.

****

Sakura was on her laptop but was having a hard time seeing the screen and her frustration was getting to her. She grabbed the laptop off her desk and pulled back her chair. The chair was on wheels that easily rolled across the cement floor of Kamiko's office that took up one corner of her museum space.

She was finally able to enter the last few codes of the seven new girls as they were being injected with their tracking devices.

A scruffy looking dog was lying in the corner watching her. She took all but the last bite of her meal and tossed it to the dog.

Aiko rubbed her inner arm remembering when Kyle removed her tracking device.

Sakura closed her laptop and headed toward the door. As Sakura did, she passed by Aiko and paused, "We even have Oksana's tracking and who knows, a year from now after her sale, when her light goes out, that will be that."

Just as Sakura began to walk away, Aiko didn't let her make one more step. Simultaneously, Aiko shifted her weight and with a straight arm across Sakura's chest, she sent Sakura off her feet, just as Sakura drew a dagger from the edge of her laptop and wielded the dagger cutting across Aiko's forearm as she was falling backwards to the floor. The laptop crashed to the floor and shattered and the room went silent.

One of the guards took a step forward to come to the aide of Sakura but Kamiko motioned for him to stay back. Sakura got up to her feet.

Kyle looked at Sakura and had only one thing to say, "Track that."

Kyle saw Aiko's arm was now bleeding and took a step toward Aiko to get in between them. Before he could, Kamiko stepped in and by hardly making any contact, she used a form of martial arts known as Aikido, and using Kyle's momentum, Kamiko had Kyle on the ground. With one hand she held his wrist, torquing his hand backward while twisting his forearm, holding him down at will.

Kamiko made her point, "This is not about you."

Kamiko let Kyle up. He worked out the kinks in his arm and wondered how she could do that so quickly with such little effort.

As one of Kamiko's students, Sakura stepped in toward Aiko with confidence. Using the dagger in her right hand as a distraction, she flinched, and with a quick step and a flick of her wrist, Sakura caught Aiko across the jaw with her left hand and as her hand came down she pulled off Aiko's necklace in a single motion.

That was the last and only full contact she made to Aiko as Aiko unleashed a quick series of blows that took Sakura out. The dog began to bark and go crazy trying to protect Sakura but his chain would let him only go so far. The guard looked at Kamiko, got a nod, then stepped in and picked Sakura up off the floor and helped her to her feet.

Pankov stepped in, picked up the necklace off the floor, and handed it back to Aiko. He then gestured to the guards and pointed to Sakura, "Take her out of here. We have business to discuss. We don't need any more distractions."

Kyle could see the clasp was broken so he held out his hand and Aiko tossed it to him. He slipped it into his front pocket for safe keeping.

As the guard exited with Sakura, Zen entered.

Kamiko called Zen over, "No more business." Kamiko felt the need to be shown a little more respect from Aiko, "Ichiro said you were a good student and a great technician of the arts. How are you as a teacher?"

Kamiko handed Zen the wakizashi then the katana to Oksana. Zen drew his sword with confidence. Oksana had yet to draw hers.

Aiko understood the point Kamiko was trying to make, "You don't have to do this. If you want to take your anger out on me, then fight me."

Each of the guards drew their weapons.

Kamiko was making sure she was in charge, "I am not angry. I'm looking to see what kind of skills you have that you have passed down to your student."

Kyle did not like where this was heading, "What are the rules?"

Aiko confirmed his worst nightmare, "There are no rules."

CHAPTER 25

Zen began to slowly advance toward Oksana. Each step he took was calculated. Most of the office was the cold cement floor but in some of the open spaces Kamiko had large floor rugs from all over the world as not only a cushion of warmth but as a kind of postcard of her travels.

Oksana firmly gripped the wooden scabbard at the top, and with her thumb pressed against the katana's hilt, released it just enough to free the tension between the katana and the scabbard. Zen screamed as his pace quickened. He raised his sword with two hands above his head.

Oksana gripped her katana with both hands and whirled her sword, using the momentum to cast the scabbard down the blade, sending the wooden protective sleeve through the air. This was a total surprise to Zen and the metal on the end of the scabbard hit him flush in the mouth stopping him in his tracks.

Oksana held herself in a defensive posture. Her heart raced as she realized she now held only the katana and for the first time, she felt what it was like to have a life-and-death moment in her own hands.

Zen quickly got a taste of his own blood. He spit out the warm crimson fluid with vengeance on his mind.

Aiko believed in Oksana but also believed in the unknown, "This is not the answer."

Kamiko believed in Zen, "I didn't hear a question." Kamiko nodded to Zen to continue.

Zen began to pace side to side a bit more cautiously. There wasn't a lot of room to maneuver. Oksana glanced at Aiko. Aiko was calm giving Oksana her trust and confidence.

Without letting go of her sword, Oksana blew the moisture from her hands. Oksana looked across the blade of her sword and tilted the blade slightly to reflect a beam of light toward Zen. It caught Zen's eyes like a wink. She wondered if she got Zen's attention this way, might it put some doubt in his mind of her skill set?

Zen turned on the ball of his foot slightly to make sure he had good footing. He lunged toward Oksana. With a burst of energy their blades clashed, as they countered a few times before they each stepped back.

A test of sorts of a few basic moves to try to find a weakness. Nothing found.

Kamiko watched as Kyle took Aiko by the hand. Aiko didn't show any emotion and Kamiko noticed that too.

Another burst of energy from Zen as he attacked. Again, their swords clashed but as they broke, Zen was able to release one hand and punch Oksana in the ribs. Oksana took a deep knee bend but her knees did not touch the floor.

Kyle felt her pain, "Oksana…"

Aiko squeezed his hand. Kyle remained quiet.

Oksana straightened up with resolve.

Zen could see she had her left arm down a bit to protect her ribs, and attacked. The ringing of the swords clashing was intense.

Zen was able to get in close enough to spit the blood from his mouth into Oksana's eyes. She was momentarily blinded. Oksana blinked out the blood as best she could but everything was a very dark blur. She found the edge of the table, almost knocking over the bowl of fruit. She tried to wipe her eyes.

Oksana fought off the panic in time to hear Zen approaching. She reached for the bowl of fruit and whirled it in Zen's direction. As the fruit fanned out from the bowl, Oksana heard the slap of Zen catching an orange. He had reached out in front of the sword's blade with his bare left hand as the rest of the fruit fell to the floor. When Zen caught the orange, it gave away his location.

Oksana didn't hesitate. She whirled the katana on target and cut the orange in half. In the process, she cut through four of Zen's fingers that were gripping the orange.

Zen was in shock. The room's silence was broken as Zen dropped the wakizashi to the floor and finally let out a scream. Zen dropped the half orange still in his hand to the floor where his fingers lie next to the other half of the orange. He tucked his bloody hand into his right arm pit to try to stop the bleeding. With his right hand, he grabbed a towel off one of the tables and wrapped what remained of his left hand. He turned toward Oksana but was stopped in his tracks by the end of Oksana's blade right in front of his face.

One of the guards trained his weapon on Oksana. Kamiko raised her hand and the guard lowered his gun. Oksana stepped back.

Zen's blood still dripped from around her eyes and she was able to see a little bit better now.

Zen stepped back and headed toward the door where one of the guards took him away to tend to his hand.

Oksana walked over, picked up the cover to her sword, and slid the blade back in along with a few drops of Zen's blood staining the inside of the scabbard forever.

Kamiko tried to hide her anger as best she could and slowed down the words to her request, "Give me the sword."

Oksana tossed the katana to Kamiko and rejoined Kyle and Aiko and was received with a big hug for her bravery.

Kamiko's tone did not hide her frustration, "Take her to one of the holding cells."

Oksana thought she had proved yourself, "But I won."

"What is it that you think you have won?"

One of the guards stepped in and led Oksana away.

Aiko could hear the confidence in Oksana's voice fade and turn to fear, "Aiko, do something."

Aiko didn't reply. Instead she leaned over and picked up the wakizashi by the handle, tossed it handle first over to Kamiko, who caught it by the handle with ease. Kamiko slipped the wakizashi back into its scabbard and put the swords back on the display stand.

Kamiko took a moment to regain her composure, "You have a fine student. Your father would have been very proud of you."

"My father was never my father. The business came first. He never talked about you. Was that by his choice or yours?"

"My brother knew his place. He accepted his role and did it well."

Kyle needed to clarify his thoughts, "He worked for you? The Masato import export business isn't a family business, it's your business."

"Yes. I learned long ago if you give a man a choice, he will believe just about anything if he thinks he will gain a substantial profit or pleasure. Once I learned that, I turned it around in my favor. Now I get pleasure from profiting off the fantasies of men and their desire to make the deal of a life time. I offer them a way to have it all."

Kyle had known Portland was one of the cities in the United States known for having the highest human trafficking rates but what he saw happening here was a whole other level.

Kamiko continued, "If I show a man he can not only have that fantasy, but he can have it at a profit, we both come out ahead."

"How does the buyer profit?" Kyle asked.

"First, I sell him the purest and untamed, then after he has had his way with her, she is returned to me for grooming. I have a place where I take the girls to become a modern-day geisha in a sense. Not the one who wears a kimono and is kept in hiding but one a man can take out on the town to give him a sense of sophistication and accomplishment."

Kyle understood, "You take the girls that are returned to you and turn them into high-end arm candy."

"Yes, and at a profit I might add."

"That you then split with the original buyer."

"When you take the oldest profession and the newest technology you get a highly marketable commodity."

Aiko felt her mind cloud and her body go numb for a moment thinking about how this was what they were going to do to Oksana, "Kyle?"

"Yes, Aiko. The plan was to sell Oksana, then eventually have her returned and taken to a facility where she would have been groomed in all things geisha."

"That is correct, Mr. Morrell," Kamiko replied. "And while the girls are in our care we teach them how to eat correctly and keep their bodies in prime shape through physical conditioning. If needed, we even offer the best in cosmetic surgery, offering them a little nip here and a tuck there to bring out the best in them."

Kyle finally saw it, what she had been talking about. He saw it in Kamiko. As Kyle was looking closely at Kamiko for any corrective surgery she may have had, he saw something else. Aiko. Her body proportions, skin tone, and the elegance in the way she walked.

Kamiko noticed the way Kyle was looking at her, "So, do you like what you see?"

"I see a woman who thinks she has it all, but has nothing."

"As you can see with your own eyes, I can have anything I want."

"But I've got the one thing that all of this can't buy," Kyle leaned forward and whispered just enough for Kamiko to pick up. "The love of your daughter."

"Believe me," Kamiko replied. "One day you will pay the price and I will be the one to collect."

Kyle felt his suspicions were confirmed when Kamiko took two fingers and thrust them just under Kyle's ribcage. Kyle was instantly out of breath and dropped to his knees.

Kamiko leaned over him, "Don't ever forget, what money can't buy, can cost you the most." Kamiko turned her back and headed over to one of the tables.

Aiko stepped in and helped Kyle to his feet, "What did you say to her?"

Kyle wasn't ready to explain, "Let it go."

Kamiko tossed the piece human pelt that was the key to the legend to Aiko, "Do you know what you are holding?"

Aiko didn't answer.

"It is the key to a treasure that my family has been searching for 200 years."

Kyle knew he was risking another paralyzing response, "So, human trafficking isn't enough for you? You're also a thief. How does a sunken treasure of a Spanish Galleon belong to you?"

"I am only taking back what is rightfully mine. One of those fishermen who saved that man was my ancestor. He took claim when he saved that man's life and was given the location of the treasure in return."

Kyle was still trying to connect dots and was not yet impressed, "But he didn't save his life. He used him as a marker. Some legacy."

"And what about yours, Mr. Morrell? Yes, I know a great deal about you and your family. Your father has been a player in our little adventure for some time now, and you let your brother die right in front of you. I guess you're proud of that."

"Who the hell do you think you are? My father may have not been the best but he was there for us when our mother died. And as far as what happened to Steven, he would have never been put in that situation if it wasn't for this so-called business of yours."

"It's in our DNA and its who we are just like in Oksana's case and makes her who she is." Kamiko regained her thought, "Our ancestors worked this land and built it with their blood so, yes, it is mine."

"Just think Aiko, one day, all of this will be yours." Kyle's sarcasm had weight that seemed to hang in the air very effectively.

Aiko made her point, "I don't want any part of this."

Kamiko did not accept her declaration, "You are already part of this and if the ship is where you say it is, you and your friends can go. If not, the girl is the first to go. She will be put up for auction and go to the highest bidder in a matter of hours."

Kamiko motioned with her hand, two guards moved in, and handcuffed Aiko and Kyle.

Kyle knew the answer to his question but asked it anyway, "And in the meantime?"

"You will be my guests."

Again, Kamiko motioned and the guards led them away.

Pankov knew he needed to be bold to get what he wanted, "The girl is mine. I will decide what happens to her..."

Pankov was interrupted as Kamiko raised her hand. Kamiko picked up the drawing of the Monarch Moon, "Once I have the Monarch Moon, we will need to eliminate all of them."

"Not the girl. Not Oksana. We had a deal."

Kamiko set down the drawing and picked up the tanto, "Fate has a way of rearing its ugly head."

Pankov slammed his hand down on the table, "You can't kill your own daughter."

In one swift move, Kamiko drew the tanto and with precision, brought the end of the blade down severing off Pankov's right pinky finger. The blade was so sharp, and with Kamiko's precise movement, Pankov didn't even feel the blade detach the end of his finger.

He did feel the thump of the end of the blade striking the table top and as quickly as the blade came down, Kamiko withdrew it. Pankov didn't know which came first, the pain from the loss of the end of his finger or the pain as his eyes told him he now was missing part of an appendage. There was a lingering moment between the two sensory overloads that hit him at once before he jerked his hand back.

Kamiko made her point, "I said, I would not kill yours."

Kamiko grabbed a small towel and wiped what little blood there was off the blade then tossed the towel to Pankov, "You better go get that looked at before you bleed all over my office."

Pankov took the towel and wrapped it tightly around his wound to try to stop the bleeding. He started to walk away dismayed at the merciless way Kamiko had a control over him, "Victor."

Pankov stopped but did not turn around.

"Aiko must never find out what my brother did to me. It is not to be her burden to bear. If I hear otherwise, next time, you will lose more than a pinky."

Pankov took that as his cue and left.

Kamiko used the tip of the blade of the tanto to flick what was left of Pankov's pinky in the direction of the dog. The dog caught the pinky in its mouth and wolfed it down.

CHAPTER 26

Pankov walked down one of the long interior hallways of the factory, past a series of rooms, clutching his right hand. The pain was becoming more tolerable but the steady throbbing of his heartbeat sent constant reminders of his actions, one after another, up his arm. Trying to resist the pain only caused his mind to relive the sins of his past. So many images and faces scrolling through his thoughts with each synchronized pulse of misery caused him to lose track of his life. One thing he thought he would never have to face were regrets and now they seemed to be flowing at will.

The dank and dingy hallway had a series of doors on either side. A few of the doors were unlocked and a couple doors were ajar giving hints to what they held inside. In one room, he could see workers processing cocaine. In the next, girls were being fitted for clothes and others getting their pictures taken to be shown to prospective buyers. Another room was stockpiled with various artillery and antipersonnel weapons. Further down he passed by holding cells.

The cells were small rooms made from wooden pallets that had been nailed together to form the walls, three pallets high by three pallets wide. On the fronts of the cells, two of the pallets were nailed together and hinged to form a door. The dirt floors were covered with old pieces of carpet. There were two girls to a cell. The conditions were filthy and each cell had a five-gallon bucket as a toilet.

There was a single mattress on the floor for the girls to share.

On the way to the end of the hall, Pankov walked on past one of the guards handing out bread and cheese through slots in the pallets to each of the girls as another handed out cups of water.

One of the girls had refused to eat and was using the extra clothes she had grabbed to make a doll out of rags. Sachi couldn't stop thinking about her sister, Mai, and sat on the floor in the back corner of the holding cell working on making the rag doll as a gift to her lost sister.

When Pankov reached the end of the hall, there were to two holding cells opposite each other made from holding pens that were at one time used for staging cattle. On one side of the hall, Aiko and Kyle were in one cell to themselves. Opposite them, Oksana was alone in her cell.

Kyle looked at Pankov and saw that his hand was wrapped in a bloody towel, "I guess negotiations for your share of the treasure didn't go well?

"You might say that."

"What more do you want from us?" Aiko added.

"Nothing, I'm here to warn you." Pankov gestured with his bloody hand, "You can't trust her, no matter what she says."

Kyle gave his obvious opinion on the matter, "No shit."

Pankov felt the pain from his hand that fed his anger, "Once she has the treasure, she will no longer need you. You only have one thing keeping you alive."

Aiko knew, "The Monarch Moon."

Pankov affirmed, "Yes."

Pankov took a long look down the hall behind him and saw that it was empty. He then turned his attention back to Aiko, "There is something you need to know, Aiko. This may not make sense at first but if you think about it, it just might explain a few things."

Before Aiko could make sense of Pankov's actions and before he could stop himself from over thinking the consequences, he just told her the truth, "Kamiko is your mother."

Kyle reached through the bars of his cell, grabbed Pankov, and pulled him in hard. Pankov broke away and gave Aiko a sincere look, "When your father became the head of the family he inherited a lot of power. Power he was not ready for. He began to over step his bounds and that included his involvement with his younger sister, Kamiko."

"You're crazy," Kyle replied, trying to protect what he already had a sense was true, and before he could go on, Aiko put her hand on his shoulder.

For Aiko, it was all starting to make sense, "That is why I was put into the orphanage. It wasn't that I had no family it was because my father was trying not to lose face."

"The first chance you get you will need to get out of here and never look back. I'll do what I can for Oksana."

Kyle was not leaving without Oksana, "That's not going to be enough."

****

President Dalton was with a couple of dignitaries from France and Canada touring the inside of the White House. It had been a long day already for the President and the group had just finished lunch on the patio.

An aide walked up to the President and pointed out it was time for a meeting.

The President excused himself and the aide continued the tour.

Dalton met up with Wintersteen and they continued on to the Oval Office.

Wintersteen closed door behind them, "How did the talks go with France and Canada?"

"Unofficially, we have a joint task force on standby in each country. They are ready to take down the shell companies the Masato's are using in each country as hubs for their human trafficking ring. Officially, the Prime Minister's birthday party was a success."

"Unofficially, do we have our men ready to go?"

"Officially, no."

CHAPTER 27

The guard had a mission and didn't bother harassing the other girls as he usually did. He made his way to the end of the hall, his sole focus, the last cell on the left. He reached a neutral space between Aiko's and Oksana's cell. The guard took a long look at Oksana, "White gold." Then the guard turned to Aiko and Kyle, "She wants the girl."

Oksana looked to Aiko.

Kyle and Aiko took a deep breath.

Pankov had a sense of confusion, "What does she want with her?"

The guard didn't answer. He unlocked Oksana's cell, put the key back in his outer jacket pocket, opened the cell door, and grabbed Oksana.

Pankov sensed the betrayal. He rushed the guard and pinned him against the cell door while he slipped his hand into the guard's pocket, "I said, what…"

The guard punched Pankov before he could finish his sentence.

The guard had an order and couldn't waste any more time on Pankov. He led Oksana away.

Pankov got to his feet and slowly began to walk away letting the guard get some distance between. The guard looked back and saw Pankov had started to follow, then turned back forward, dragging Oksana along.

Pankov knew the day would come when he would have to make a choice. He glanced back and saw what Aiko and Kyle already knew, they were all pawns in someone else's game that had no rules, no trust, and no honor.

Kyle had to ask, "What did he mean by white gold?"

"Some of these girls can be worth their weight in gold, especially the fair-skinned ones. Like gold, the purer, the better. Or in Oksana's case, royalty."

"What are you talking about?" Kyle asked.

"Oksana's mother, Karina, came from a long line of Russian royalty. The Romanov's, decedents of Peter the Great. That's why I traded five of my top girls to get her."

Kyle could not grasp the lack of humanity that came with human trafficking, "You traded five girls for your wife?"

"Of course, she was not my wife at the time, she was only fifteen and I was taking a chance."

"A chance at what?"

"That she was still a virgin. I was a very lucky man, royal blood or not, I wanted her pure and to blossom into a beautiful woman. I see a lot of her beauty in Oksana and that's why I was so disappointed when I found out she was not mine." Pankov turned back to Kyle and without malice tore into Kyles heart, "That's why I was able to request top dollar for her. Being of royal blood and all."

Kyle was so enraged he began shaking the hell out of the cell door trying to test the strength of the lock and break it open.

"I am not your enemy," Pankov tossed the keys to the cell he had taken from the guard in the struggle. The keys came to a sliding stop just outside their cell door.

Pankov looked at Aiko, "You should be more worried about things closer to home. Kamiko will stop at nothing to get what she wants." He raised his right hand and showed Aiko and Kyle his bloody hand.

****

The guard used his size to whisk Oksana down the hall and didn't seem to care that he was practically bouncing her off the walls along the way.

Oksana saw an opportunity to let her feelings be known for the mishandling of her. As the guard was about to go through the door to Kamiko's office, Oksana stopped resisting and threw what weight she had back his way. With her shoulder, she was able to get the guard off stride to make him lose his balance just enough to cause him to catch his shoulder on the doorjamb with authority. Oksana got a kick out of it but the guard didn't hesitate and with a quick shove, rammed Oksana into the other doorjamb. Oksana knew she was going to get a good bruise but she felt it was worth it and thought, "Oh, yeah. That's going to leave a mark."

When Oksana entered the room, an older man in a white-linen suit carrying a leather satchel, passed her on his way out.

She saw Kamiko had moved away a partition and was standing by a large steel safe that was open and about the size of a refrigerator.

"Come here, Oksana. I want to show you something very rare."

Oksana approached Kamiko.

Kamiko showed her a coin she had just acquired, "This is a nineteen thirty-three double eagle. This twenty-dollar gold coin is only one of a few that are still in existence. It is one of the rarest coins in the world."

"Why do you need a safe if it is only worth twenty dollars?"

"Because, now it is worth seven and a half million dollars."

Oksana reached out to hold the coin but Kamiko turned and placed the coin in its clear plastic container on the middle shelf of the safe.

Oksana saw that where Kamiko placed the coin there was a large diamond in a sealed glass jar. But what really got her attention was an old sword leaning up on one of the inner walls of the safe, "And that sword, how much is it worth?"

The sword was about thirty-seven inches long, had silver threads entwining the handle with silver and gold details on the hilt. What was left of the Latin inscription was barely visible and there was a faint image of a hand holding a cross on the pommel.

"That was recovered from the bottom of a lake in Northern Europe. It is a Nordic sword that most likely went down during a Viking funeral."

"How did it end up on the bottom of a lake?"

"When someone of high stature died, they put him in a boat, set it a drift, then shot flaming arrows into the boat lighting it on fire. Eventually, what was left sank to the bottom."

"And how did you get it?"

"I am a collector and I like to acquire nice things."

"Coins, swords…diamonds?"

"That is not just any diamond. That is a very special family heirloom."

"How much is it worth?"

"It is priceless, like a lot of things in this vault and in this room."

Kamiko closed the safe, spun the tumbler, and replaced the partition.

"I have a question for you, Oksana. Do you think Zen deserved to have his fingers cut off in such a way?"

Oksana thought to herself, "Yes."

Kamiko picked up the katana and finished wiping the small traces of blood off the blade, slid the blade back into its scabbard, and then set it upon the display stand.

"I can see the bond that you have with Kyle and Aiko. That makes you very valuable to me."

Kamiko removed the necklace she was wearing and put it around Oksana's neck.

"This is a very special necklace. It is made from green obsidian. I only collect the rarest and most beautiful."

Oksana had sensed she just became a collectible.

****

Aiko and Kyle slowly and quietly made their way down the hall unlocking the cell doors. They motioned to the girls to wait in their cells.

One of the girls came from behind them and took off running down the hall.

Kyle reached out but could not grab the girl in time, "Wait…"

Aiko started to go after her.

Just as she caught up to her at the end of the hall, they turned a blind corner together, and Aiko ran into Sakura pinning the young girl between them.

Sakura was in a dress and heels pulling an overnight piece of luggage. As Aiko stepped back, Sakura gripped the luggage handle and swung it up at Aiko.

Aiko ducked and pushed the young girl aside. As the luggage passed overhead she used the momentum to push Sakura in the opposite direction.

Sakura was now out of position as Aiko grabbed her from behind with a choke hold. Sakura struggled for a moment and passed out from the hold.

Kyle came up behind Aiko, "Looks like Kamiko was sending her out of town."

"She must have a car waiting."

Kyle cautiously walked up ahead, looked into the open bay, then returned, "Looks like they have a truck heading back to the docks and she was planning on catching a ride."

"We need to be on that truck."

"We can't leave Oksana."

"I know where the Monarch Moon is. If we get it first, we will have the power to trade it for Oksana."

"You're willing to do that? Risk everything on a treasure that has been lost for over 200 years? How do we know it even exists?"

"Because, it is not where she says it is. Now help me get Sakura out of these clothes."

Kyle paused momentarily to digest what Aiko had just said, then he helped Aiko take Sakura into a nearby room.

****

The room at one time must have been a control room for the factory as the walls were made of concrete. It had been cleared out of all the desk and cabinets and was now used as a storage room to hold many kinds of ordinance. Unmarked crates were piled all around the room with a few that appeared to have been opened recently. As Aiko was finishing getting dressed. Kyle took a look around the room and thought these walls would not be standing, concrete or not, if for any reason one of these crates exploded.

187

It would cause a chain reaction of force that would cause this factory to go nuclear.

Kyle saw a small wooden case with a sprayed-on label that read, G-17, and opened it. He thought, "It couldn't be." As he opened the box he felt his heart drop like it was Christmas. A Glock 17 9mm compact pistol.

He removed the Glock and it felt good to hold the polymer grip in his hand. It was like meeting up with an old friend. He removed the clip, checked to see if it was full, and sent all fifteen rounds home. Kyle flashed his new toy in Aiko's direction with a smile. Now he was excited to see what else Santa had in store for him. He placed the Glock in the small of his back then cautiously opened another box. This one was a little larger and inside were a dozen Claymore mines. He opened another box and found blasting caps, a hundred-feet of electric firing wire, and a detonator.

"I think I just found part of our exit strategy."

Aiko had finished putting on the dress and was having a hard time putting on the three-inch heels. She reached out to brace herself. In doing so, she leaned on the open luggage bag. She felt a large manila envelope. She opened it and inside was a set of container documents.

"And I think I found out a way onto the docks."

CHAPTER 28

Aiko walked out of the ordinance room wearing Sakura's outfit and shoes. She found the three-inch heels to be a bit awkward.

Kyle followed Aiko as they headed toward the waiting truck.

Kyle motioned for the girls to come out of their cells. They began to file out one by one. As the girls came closer Aiko heard someone approaching. Kyle and Aiko stepped back into the room and closed the door just as the guard walked around the corner. The first girl the guard saw as Sachi. She was so frightened she dropped her rag doll and began to walk backwards. The girls slowly began to retreat to their cells, all but Sachi, she took a stance and refused to go back inside that hell hole.

The guard didn't mind disciplining the girls, in a way, he enjoyed it.

Kyle had opened the door to the room he had retreated to without making any noise and was just in time to see the guard grab Sachi by the hair.

Kyle looked down and saw the rag doll Sachi had dropped.

Sachi could feel a clump of her hair being pulled so hard it almost lifted her off the ground. She was just about to scream when, suddenly, she was released.

Sachi looked up and saw the guard with a blank look on his face, drop to his knees then watched his body drop to the floor dead. Back over by the door, Kyle was holding her rag doll over the end of his Glock's muzzle having used the doll as a silencer.

Aiko then motioned for the girls to head off in different directions.

Guards in the open bay had seen some of the commotion and started after the girls that had escaped.

Aiko, dressed as Sakura, calmly walked toward the truck with the suitcase in tow.

The driver of the 5-ton tactical vehicle was wearing his thick glasses and was having a cigarette while reading his newspaper. He glanced up from under the rim of his hat and saw his passenger coming, put out his cigarette, and hopped in the truck.

Aiko walked around to the passenger side of the large vehicle, and as she did, she lifted a part of the camouflaged heavy tarpaulin but really couldn't see anything at a glance. Aiko climbed into the passenger seat and as soon as she looked up, the driver realized it was not Sakura. He turned to get out of the truck and go for help just as Kyle was approaching. Before the driver could react, Kyle clocked him with a right cross, knocking him out.

In all the commotion, there wasn't anyone really paying attention to Kyle and Aiko. Kyle was able to drag the driver's body behind a nearby crate without being noticed.

Kyle climbed into the truck and got behind the wheel wearing the driver's glasses and hat.

"What do you think?"

"You don't look Japanese."

"Let's hope the guard at the gate has worse eyesight than this guy, but I doubt it."

Kyle fired up the Cummins diesel, put the truck in gear, and they headed out.

****

Kamiko was looking over her notes on the treasure's location that she had carefully fanned out on her desk.

Oksana was in a chair at the end of the table, looking at a map showing a chain of islands labeled: NuFu-23, as one of the guards entered.

"What is it?" Kamiko didn't like being interrupted.

"They have escaped."

Kamiko turned to the guard giving her full attention, "Who's escaped?"

"All of them. All of the cell doors have been unlocked."

Oksana's eyes lit up with a sense of hope.

Kamiko's mind calculated time and distance, "They couldn't have gotten far. Alert the gate. Find the American and bring him to me. He will be the first one I make an example of."

Oksana's eyes now tell a different story.

The 5-ton truck Kyle and Aiko had acquired was following within the orange and white polyethylene 42-inch traffic barrels that narrowed the four lanes down to two and slowed down vehicles as they approached the exit side of the gate.

The phone rang inside the guard shack. The guard answered the phone as the truck stopped outside the shack.

The guard put down the phone and saw Aiko behind the wheel holding out a set of papers in her left hand. What he couldn't see was the Glock Aiko had in her right hand below the edge of the window pointed at the guard.

He didn't look at the papers, but instead, stepped up onto the runner and poked his head into the truck looking for the American. As he did, Aiko covered the Glock with the papers. He only saw Aiko. Aiko could tell from the guard's attempt at intimidation that he knew something wasn't right.

The guard stepped back off the runner and Aiko could see that he already had his hand on his gun that he wore in the holster on his hip. The tension on Aiko's trigger finger was an adrenalized heartbeat away from taking out the guard. At that same moment, Kyle had circled the truck and was waiting for him. Kyle got the guard in a choke hold from behind, pulled a knife from the guard's utility belt, and stabbed him from behind, piercing his lung, taking him out with a silent kill.

Aiko and Kyle both heard the noise. It was the phone. As the truck approached, the guard had set down the phone, leaving it off the receiver. They could hear a man's voice on the other end yelling in Japanese as Kyle hung up the phone.

Kyle removed a set of keys from the guard's belt, "We don't have much time." Kyle thumbed through the keys and spotted one that went to the Jeep that was parked just outside the shack. He tossed the keys to Aiko and Aiko gave Kyle the small suitcase. Kyle set the suitcase on the fender of the truck, unzipped it, and began going over the contents of Claymore mines, wire, and a detonator.

****

Kamiko watched Oksana as she paced around her office scanning the art and how she subconsciously couldn't stop fondling the necklace Kamiko and given to her. One of the paintings was behind a pane of glass and Oksana was able to see her reflection and saw how the necklaced looked on her.

Kamiko's comment startled Oksana out of her trance, "Being that it is one of a kind, it is priceless,"

"Then how did you pay for it?"

Kamiko looked around the room at a few pieces of art on display hanging on the walls.

"The cost is what you are willing to sacrifice for and to give of yourself to keep it."

"So, you're a thief."

193

"I can live with that. One day you will understand the value of things and the value you place on your happiness."

Kamiko gestured to a painting, "Take this painting here by Rembrandt. It's called Storm on the Sea of Galilee. It was stolen from an art Museum in Boston in nineteen-ninety by two men posing as police officers. Does that make me a thief? If it hangs on this wall it is worthless. That is, until there is someone willing to pay for it. You will find everything has value."

"Forty thousand dollars."

Kamiko gave Oksana a quizzical look.

Oksana finished her thought, "That is my value. That is the price that Victor was willing to sell me to a man named Marcus for, that is, until my mother killed him."

"Oh, little one. You are worth so much more."

CHAPTER 29

Off in the distance, two Jeeps were heading toward the guard shack.

As they got closer the lanes narrowed. The driver of the first Jeep could see the arm of the wooden gate was still down so he pulled up alongside the right side of the idling truck in the outer lane. The second Jeep stopped, just off the back-right bumper, blocking in the 5-ton.

The two men from the first Jeep noticed the guard on duty's body was lying on the ground out in front of the empty truck just beyond the gate. They stood up in their open Jeep to get a better look. This caused the two men in the second Jeep to do the same.

All four men drew their weapons and slowly began to scan the area from their Jeeps. One of them eventually noticed there was a wire on the ground running from one of the orange and white traffic drums to the next, along the entire length of both Jeeps, and along the three-foot cement K-rail barrier wall.

The guard pointed to the wire as he tapped the shoulder of the man next to him but it was too late.

Kyle and Aiko were down behind the other side of the cement barriers opposite the barrels. Kyle cranked on the detonator handle and all the Claymore mines that had been placed under each of the orange and white traffic barrels went off simultaneously.

After the dust cleared, Kyle and Aiko hopped over the cement barrier and inspected the damage the Claymores had done. The Jeep nearest to them had been flipped on its side and its occupants were nowhere in sight. Aiko looked at the Jeep that had been behind the 5-ton and it was peppered with frag from the Claymores. Aiko knelt and looked under the Jeep and could see the two men had been blown out of their Jeep and their unidentifiable bodies were painting the roadway crimson.

Kyle saw a large hole in the side of the 5-ton's camouflaged tarpaulin and climbed on the turned-up Jeep to get a better look. He cautiously peered into the back of the truck through the massive hole and saw both men's bodies disfigured from the Claymores. One man had died instantly as he was practically cut in half from the blast. The other guard was barely alive.

His shrapnel riddled body had been blown out of the Jeep and through the tarp that covered the sides of the truck. The man's mind was so detached from his body that he had to look at his mangled hand to see if he was holding his radio close enough his face to try to call for help. Kyle recognized the man as the guard who now possessed his cell phone.

It was very quiet in Kamiko's office when a squawk came over Kamiko's radio and she replied, "Yes, what is it?"

Over the radio came a breathless reply, "They are… at the gate…"

Oksana saw a fire burning in Kamiko like a lit fuse, and smiled.

Kamiko demanded action, "Stop them! Do not let them get off this site. Do you copy?"

There was no reply.

"Do you copy?"

Again, no answer.

The squawk on the radio died.

Kamiko saw Oksana smiling, "What are you smiling at? They left you."

Oksana lost her smile.

The guard made one last effort to call for help over his radio. The guard's mind was startled when he saw the barefoot foreigner standing in front of him and his intentions were to try to shoot the gaijin, but his body would not do as it was asked.

The guard saw his gun had been tossed to the side from the blast and out of instinct, he went for it. He dropped the radio and with what energy he could muster, he tried to reach for his gun but to no avail. It was just too far away for his riddled body. But in his mind, he would not give in so instead, he pointed his index finger at Kyle as if he was holding the gun. Kyle climbed in the truck, picked up the man's gun, put one round in the chamber, and removed the clip.

Cautiously, Kyle moved in close enough to the man while holding the gun on him, and reached into the front pocket of the man's shirt to retrieve his cell phone.

The phone fell apart in his hand from taking a direct hit from the shrapnel of the Claymore.

Kyle slowly backed away. He then tossed the gun in the man's lap and said, "Use it wisely." Kyle climbed off the Jeep and pointed to the other Jeep on the other side of the guard shack. As they drove away, Kyle and Aiko could hear the distinct short echo of a single round being discharged.

CHAPTER 30

The Jeep Kyle and Aiko were in merged onto the paved road into traffic from off the dusty side road that led away from the factory.

They passed a road sign that read: PORT OF NIIGATA.

Kyle was driving. Aiko had the papers from Sakura's suitcase in hand.

Kyle was still a little apprehensive about Aiko's plan, "Are you sure about this? They could take Oksana and be gone before we get back."

"They are not going to run. They will be coming after us. That is why we have to get to the treasure and retrieve the stone before they do."

"What if the location is wrong or the treasure is just a myth, then what?"

"You do not preserve the hide of the yakuza with cryptic art or put elaborate clues on the side of a set of swords for a myth."

****

The work along the docks at the port of Niigata was slowing down as most of the crew that worked the day shift were leaving. Dock workers were changing shifts and the smaller night crew was coming on.

The guards at the gate were doing their routine hellos and goodbyes as Kyle pulled up in the Jeep. The security guard said something in Japanese that Kyle did not understand. Aiko reached across and handed of the guard some papers. The guard took a glance at the papers then at Kyle and Aiko.

After a moment, the guard handed them back the papers, pointed off in the distance, and mumbled something else in Japanese Kyle didn't understand, but Kyle nodded as if he did, then drove on.

Kyle thought so far so good, "Now what?"

"We need to find a boat with sonar that can handle a day at sea."

"How far away is the treasure and in how deep of water?"

"I don't know."

Kyle stopped the Jeep.

Aiko continued, "All I know is the approximate location and that there will be a marker."

"What kind of marker?"

"The swords revealed that the Monarch Moon would be marked by death and it is located one-mile North West of Sado Island."

"That is a lot of area to cover."

Aiko opened the envelope from which she held the cargo shipping manifest and produced a map of the ocean around Sado Island with a small area circled just North West of the island.

"It looks like Kamiko was sending Sakura here to meet someone to take her to this location. There seems to be a set of reefs along this area."

"That would make sense. A ship lost in the storm, not knowing the area, runs aground and sinks along with its cargo." Kyle looked at Aiko with trust and conviction, "Let's find us a boat."

****

A beautiful 47-foot Riviera G2 sport Fisher yacht has just docked and a deckhand was checking the moorings as the owner of the yacht and three of his party guests were disembarking.

The owner gave the dock worker a few commands in Japanese then with a drunken toss, threw the yacht keys toward the worker and the keys hit the worker in the head and then landed on the deck. The party goers found this amusing. The group then headed up the dock toward the restaurant for dinner and another round of drinks.

Aiko and Kyle were within ear shot.

Aiko knew there wasn't much time, "I think this is our boat. The man just told the worker the boat had already been refueled and he was leaving the keys for him to take it over to his personal slip."

"And here I thought valet service was only for cars. Silly me."

"You are not a silly man, Kyle Morrell."

Aiko walked away and headed toward the yacht leaving Kyle to ponder her last statement. Kyle followed, giving Aiko room as she approached the dock worker. Kyle watched Aiko as she seemed to be negotiating with the dock worker and handed him a piece of paper.

The dock worker took the paper and left.

Kyle watched the worker pass then joined Aiko, "And just like that we have a boat?"

"The documents that gave us access to the docks are also like keys to the container itself. Whoever has the document owns the contents. The worker was treated unfairly so I offered him the contents of one of the shipping containers if he could take a long break."

Aiko turned and was about to board the yacht then stepped and turned back to Kyle, "You can drive this boat?"

"Yes."

Aiko turned and boarded. As she did she mocked Kyle loud enough for Kyle to hear her, "Silly me."

From a distance, the half Asian, half American man, casually dressed, with a small pair of binoculars was watching Aiko board the yacht.

He looked at his watch and made note of the time. Again, he looked through binoculars and watched Kyle undo the ropes releasing the yacht from the pier, then as he jumped aboard, started the yacht, and got the boat underway.

The man put away his notes to get out a cell phone. He spoke in perfect English, "I have eyes on them, Sir." The man listened, nodded to the voice on the other end of the phone, then replied, "A yacht called, SAISHO NO CHI."

CHAPTER 31

The SAISHO NO CHI's name on the hull of the yacht was pristine like the rest of the boat.

The waves crashed away from the bow of the boat as it traveled through the water at 20 knots. Then the boat's engines revved and were cut off. The water around the yacht calmed as it drifted to a stop.

Kyle was at the helm with Aiko by his side.

The boat's Garmin GPS sonar equipment showed the boat's coordinates and depth of the shelf below them on its 10-inch monitor.

Kyle looked at Aiko's paperwork and then at the monitor, "I think we're close. The shelf is right where you said it would be. All we have to do is find a marker or the outline of a 200-year-old wreck."

The sun was starting to set.

Aiko took a look off into the distance and saw the sun beginning to set on the horizon, "I think we are not going to find it tonight."

Kyle hit the toggle to drop the yacht's anchor.

****

The floor of the ocean's shelf was covered in beautiful coral of many colors and shapes.

The anchor hit the ocean floor causing the sediment to stir and as the yacht drifted, the anchor dragged momentarily until it became caught on the edge of the coral reef.

As the waters cleared, an unagi, or Japanese eel, was swimming along the coral. Everything was picturesque and tranquil, that is, until what looked to be the form of bones of a human leg appeared. The silver eel began nibbling on and around some of sponges and sea anemones that were clinging to the bone as it scavenged over the sea life that had taken over the bones.

The eel worked its way along what was left of the human remains. The form of a full size human skeleton that had been lodged into the coral began to take shape. Over the years, the coral and the skeleton have become one. The lavish looking coral had decorated the bones, giving the skeleton an appearance of a man who lived as colorfully in life, as well as in death.

****

One of the features of the interior of the yacht's stateroom was a fish tank that doubled as mood lighting in the sleeping quarters. The large tank was stocked with coral and colorful stones and was just as impressive as the ocean's shelf below.

Aiko's hand passed over the outside of the front of the aquarium's glass.

Her hand passed by one of two triggerfish in the tank and the aggressive fish made an attempt to bite her hand through the glass and it quickly swam away.

Kyle walked up behind Aiko. His arms enveloped her.

Aiko leaned back into him as Kyle kissed her on the neck.

Aiko was trying to relax but her thoughts were elsewhere, "I'm worried about tomorrow."

"We get the Monarch Moon first and that will give us the leverage we need to get Oksana and get away from here all together."

"I want to believe you."

"Then believe me. Together we can do whatever we want, wherever we want."

"Why do you have such faith in me? I am not a woman who can love you the way you want me to."

"I would hope you would know by now that what I feel for you is something I've never known, and that is good enough for me."

"Good enough is not what love is."

Aiko started to walk away. Kyle never let go of her hand.

He guided her over to the bed, "I may not have the right words to explain to you how you make me feel so let me tell you this way."

Aiko turned toward Kyle and saw his eyes, his intentions.

Her eyes began to water from the pure emotion that she felt as he offered her his heart and soul. Aiko drifted onto the bed and Kyle followed like a magnet naturally being drawn into the same space. He willfully fell into her grace.

The triggerfish were at the edge of the tank seemingly watching.

On the glass of the tank, there was a muted reflection of Kyle removing Aiko's pants, and as he kept his eyes on Aiko he let her pants aimlessly fall to the floor.

Together Kyle and Aiko caressed and entwined with each other as one and their passion was shared without words.

Aiko's eyes were no longer sad but full of passion as Kyle moved up along her body and in doing so, left a series of light kisses telling her everything he could about how much he loved her in each kiss.

Now face-to-face, Kyle raised one brow and smiled.

Aiko returned the smile, "Tell me more."

The triggerfish seemed to react simultaneously as if they had seen too much and scurried away.

The comforter on the bed that was made of velvet fabric had a paisley gold and tan design that matched the rustic European look of the headboard. In the dim lighting, Kyle saw how Aiko's tan skin blended with the cover, and in his mind, was just as soft. Kyle could feel his heart pounding sending the passion he felt for Aiko riding the adrenaline that was passing through his entire body.

Aiko could feel the power and roughness in Kyle's hands as he pulled her body closer. They rolled across the bed and Aiko ended up on top. Her inner thighs could feel the roughness of his jeans. She ran her hands slowly down over his chest and without pausing went right for his belt buckle. As soon as she had it undone, Kyle rolled Aiko over and stood up next to the bed. So many thoughts had been running through his head all day and now he could only focus on one thing, how beautiful Aiko was.

Kyle removed his jeans and underwear as one then tossed them next to Aiko's.

Aiko climbed up to the top of the bed and slipped under the comforter. Kyle wasn't having any of that and removed the comforter from the bed altogether. Aiko then pulled down the sheets halfway and slipped her feet under and before she could straighten out her legs, Kyle grabbed the top sheet and pulled it all the way down.
Kyle wanted nothing in the way of him seeing all of Aiko as they made love.

Aiko patted her hand on the white linen and Kyle sat on the edge of the bed. Aiko moved in behind him and kissed his neck, wrapped her arms around him, then her legs. Kyle could feel her breasts against his back.

He turned and with one arm grabbed her around the waist and with her legs still wrapped around him he guided her body around to the front so she ended up facing him, sitting on his lap.

They kissed like it was their last kiss. They made love like it was their last time.

Kyle was at the stern of the yacht sitting in a swivel chair with a fishing rod off the back. He had a pair of binoculars at his feet.

He took a moment to let his mind wonder and it kept coming back to, "How did I end up in the Sea of Japan on this fine morning?"

Aiko came up from the stateroom and joined him, "Do you really think you're going to catch a fish without using line or a reel?"

The pole Kyle had off the stern in fact had no reel.

"It's just for show. That vessel off in the distance is the RAISA. It passed by at a safe distance. It looks to be some sort of research vessel. I want them to think we are actually out here having a good time."

"Are you having a good time?"

"I am now. Take a look at the Garmin. There seems to be more than just fish down there."

Aiko looked at the sonar screen.

Kyle had captured a freeze frame of the shelf below, "Follow the line down to the anchor. Now off to the right." There was a faint designation on the ocean shelf.

A "V" at one end and a closed bracket shape to the right with two faint lines across the middle.

Aiko had a good idea of what it could be, "It looks like two chopsticks on a broken plate."

"I think those two chopsticks are what's left of the ship's masts laying across the outline of the bow of a 200-year-old shipwreck."

"Kyle, we found it!"

"Maybe. Don't get too excited. More than one ship may have fallen prey to this reef."

Kyle picked up the binoculars and took another look at the RAISA's stern as it seemed to be heading away.

Kyle turned his chair around toward Aiko, who leaned over, and pulled back a tarp exposing two sets of diving gear.

"Where did all of this come from?"

"I saw a couple of diving tanks strapped to the inside panel and figured there had to be more. So, I looked around in the storage cabinets and found two sets of everything. We've even got a pair of wet suits. Looks like one will fit me okay. The other might be a little big on you but should do the trick. Would you like to take a better look at that ship?"

CHAPTER 32

Bubbles from the ocean floor rose the 50 feet to the surface as the morning sunlight danced across it. The sun's rays reached into the water illuminating it with a warm yellow which added to the deep blue of the ocean's depths and caused the water near the surface to appear to soften to a light green.

The underwater cathedral ceiling was breached as Kyle and Aiko broke the surface. They checked their gauges and dive gear before descending.

Kyle and Aiko dove, following the anchor's chain. Halfway down, Aiko grabbed onto the chain and paused so she could look back up toward the surface. The sun pierced the veil of the surface with parallel beams of light that diminished the deeper they cut through the cool water on down to shallow coral shelf below.

Kyle touched her shoulder to get her attention. She gave him a thumbs up that she was okay and they continued the dive.

When they reached the shelf, Kyle and Aiko both turned on their hand-held lights. They both saw it through the dancing kelp at the same time, the leg of a human skeleton covered in coral of many vibrant colors. Kyle brushed his hand up along the leg trying to trace where the rest of the body should be.

It was all there, just hidden in calcified coral that had attached itself to the skeleton over many years.

Aiko saw where the chest cavity was open below the ribs and started to touch the breastplate when a large silver eel swam out from inside the skeleton giving them both a fright. The eel slowly serpentined around, as if on guard, then with a quick whip of its body scurried away.

Kyle looked down over the length of the skeleton and figured the body had to be about six feet tall, so was probably a man. Something caught his eye near one of the feet. A chain was attached around the ankle that went down into the sediment. Kyle pulled up on it and pulled up a ballast stone that was attached to the other end. He gently set the stone back down trying not to disturb any more debris than needed as not to dirty the water.

Kyle and Aiko gave each other a nod then Kyle pointed with an open hand to head off over to a nearby ridge-line, just passed the coral reef in what he thought to be the direction of the remains of the 200-year-old Spanish Galleon, the AMADA.

Along the way, they each found bits and pieces of debris that when they picked it up, disintegrated in their hands. Aiko stopped to look at something wedged in a piece of coral. When she looked up, she saw that Kyle was about thirty yards ahead, holding his position. She started heading his way and the closer she got, the large dark shadow off in the distance became clearer. It was an outline of a ship.

As they swam over to the remains of the ship, there appeared to be nothing at all remaining. The entire ship had collapsed onto itself over the years and the ship's two masts had fallen forward toward the bow. They moved sand side to side and found nothing. They tried another part of the ship and found a breach in the ship's deck and looked inside. Nothing.

After about 45 minutes of trying to find any sign of proof that this was indeed the AMADA, Kyle checked his gauge then pointed to Aiko to surface.

At the surface, bubbles burst as they breached alongside the yacht, followed by Kyle and Aiko, as they rose up through their expended air bubbles. Each removed their regulators and masks.

Aiko felt the same thing Kyle did, "It is all gone. That wreck has been picked clean."

"Maybe it is not the AMADA?"

"You saw that skeleton. The clues said it would be marked by death. I'll bet that is the pirate Kamiko was talking about."

"If that's the case, why the legend of the Monarch Moon and going through all of these elaborate details to hide its whereabouts if it has already been discovered?"

Pankov's voice came from above, "Because after 200 years, the one story that still lives on, the Monarch Moon was never recovered."

Kyle and Aiko looked up to see Pankov on board the yacht flanked by a guard holding a gun on them. Behind them on the other side of the yacht was the RAISA with lines attached to the SAISHO NO CHI holding her position.

At the stern of the yacht, Pankov's guard had Kyle and Aiko at gun point as they finished removing the scuba gear.

Pankov picked up a bag amongst the gear and opened it, "Nothing."

Aiko played into his hand, "I am thinking you already knew that."

"Thought as much. Over time, the ancestors have known about this site and plundered it for all it was worth, and it was worth a lot. That treasure is what the Masato Empire has become."

Kyle was feeling a bit defeated and worried about Oksana, "So why all of this for a single stone?"

"Because it has never been found."

Kyle looked at the water in the area from where they just emerged, "Who's to say it ever existed? Maybe the pirate was just making up the story to save his own skin."

"So now there is a pirate? I thought this was all a story? Which is it?"

Aiko confirmed, "Yes, there was a pirate. We found the marker."

Pankov inquired, "Where is it then?"

Aiko moved to the back of the stern, leaned over the back, and with her right hand braced herself as she pointed overboard with her left.

The guard next to her turned to take a look over the edge of the yacht. In doing so, took his eye off of Aiko. Aiko grabbed the six-foot fishing rod Kyle was using as a decoy out of its holder and pulled it apart into two halves.

The guard turned back and it was too late for him to react as Aiko used the two halves of the rod as weapons and began to punish the guard, striking him into submission using the three-foot fiberglass rods like fighting sticks.

It all happened so fast no one had time to react, that is, all except Pankov as he drew his gun.

Everyone else had to stand by as Pankov let the fight continue as punishment for his guard for letting Aiko get the best of him. The guard was able to make it to his feet and took a step back to get his bearings from the beat-down. The man looked at his arms and saw the many welts that Aiko had bestowed upon him. The guard felt the rage of anger build from the attack as well as at Pankov for letting the assault continue. The man wanted payback and picked up a loose piece of rope that was used to tie down the air tanks. He wrapped it around his hands like one would hold a garrote. He took one step toward Aiko and she let the barrage continue. Aiko caught him on the way in with a couple of blows but his size and strength allowed him to power through the attack.

The guard was able to block Aiko's right forearm with his left as he came into Aiko's body with blow from his right.

The punch caught Aiko flush and for an instant the pain in her gut weakened her legs but she held her ground. The guard was able to get alongside Aiko and he quickly tried to get the rope around her neck. As Aiko saw the rope coming, she put the larger end of the fishing pole up near her neck and the rope caught onto it on the way to her throat. Aiko could feel the man's power and knew she only had seconds to react. Aiko used her feet to kick off one of the support posts to push her and her assailant backwards. As the two of them stumbled back, Kyle stuck out his foot and tripped the man, causing them both to lose their balance. They crashed hard against the mahogany hand rail that lined the back of both sides of the stern. The blow almost knocked the man out allowing Aiko to get away from his grasp and the rope from around her neck.

Aiko was able to catch her breath but the fight was not over, the guard awkwardly made his way to his feet, and only seemed more vengeful. Aiko was ready and raised her fighting rods once more. The guard knew he needed protection. He saw a couple of life preservers, picked them up, and wrapped them around his forearms as armor. What he didn't see was that Aiko had reattached the two halves of the fishing rod back together. When the man came at her again, she whipped the entire length of the rod with the full execution of swinging a katana and caught the man flush on the side of his face.

The contact was so violent, it sliced open his skin along his jaw line and froze him in his tracks. The pain of it kicked in and the man dropped to his knees.

Aiko turned to go after Pankov but he already had his gun trained on her. Kyle stepped in front of her as a shield.

The guard on the ground reached for his gun but before he could pick it up Aiko whacked the back of his hand with one end of the fishing rod leaving a welt that included the shape of the metal eyelet off the end of the rod.

Pankov interjected, "That's enough."

Aiko dropped the fishing rod.

Pankov laid out the options, "I'm trying to make this as simple as possible, either you tell me where the Monarch Moon is or we sell the girl to the highest bidder."

Kyle and Aiko followed Pankov's gaze and looked up onto the research vessel. There, looking over the rail was Oksana and behind her was, Kamiko.

CHAPTER 33

Aboard the RAISA, in the sitting area at the stern, Pankov had Kyle, Aiko, Dr. Akihito, and his wife Raisa. All of them under the watchful eye of two of his guards at gun point.

Kyle had to let a smirk out as he looked at one of the guards who was covering his welts. The more prominent ones were on the back of his hand, there was one on his neck, and two across his face.

Raisa stood up and headed toward the ship's galley. One of the guards held her up momentarily, "Where do you think you're going?"

"To the galley. Not to worry, I'll bring you back some water, too."

The guard hesitated then allowed her to go on her way.

Inside the galley, Kamiko wanted the room alone to think and sent the guard that was with her on a quest, "Go get the girl and meet me on the deck."

The guard did as he was told.

A minute later, Raisa entered the galley and was not surprised to see Kamiko waiting for her.

Kamiko confirmed their plans were on schedule, "Is everything in order, Raisa?"

"Yes. The helicopter is standing by."

"Does Akihito suspect anything?"

"No. All he cares about is his funding. As far as he knows, the grants you supply for him to make his explorations possible are in my control, he is happy."

"Very good, Raisa. When this is all over we will rendezvous as scheduled. I better get back to our guests."

Kamiko left the galley and headed up to the stern. Raisa stayed behind to gather up a few snacks from the cupboards and some cold bottles of water from the mini-fridge before she headed back up herself.

Kamiko took her place on the deck as the center of attention. She then motioned the guard to release Oksana in her direction. Kamiko put her arm around Oksana's shoulder to help Oksana keep her balance as the water had a little chop to it. The staff quickly finished their duties cleaning up the area, then left. Raisa appeared from the ship's galley bringing a tray of food and water.

Kamiko walked up to Aiko and Kyle, "Mr. Morrell, you have a choice to make. I guess it will come down to what you are willing to do."

Aiko made it clear, "There is nothing left on the AMADA."

"Then there is no reason to keep you two around."

The guard with the welts stepped in toward Kyle as he was calculating a plan, "I think I know where it is."

Kamiko did not want to waste any more time, "Tell me."

Kyle looked around and took a second to assess the situation.

He saw one of the servants had a familiar face. He couldn't remember where he had seen this man before. It was only a glance and, as it turned out, it was the man at the marina on the radio, Hamamoto.

Kamiko grabbed Oksana tightly by the back of the neck causing Oksana to whimper, "I'm waiting and I won't ask again."

"We will need assurances," Kyle replied.

The guard with the welts, without warning, stabbed Kyle with a diver's knife in his side, between his hip his rib cage.

Kyle was in shock from the pain and could barely understand what the guard said, "There's your assurance. Now go get it."

The guard grabbed Kyle in his weakened state and tossed him overboard.

Without hesitation, Aiko dove over the side of the yacht after Kyle.

Kyle was sinking toward the bottom as Aiko quickly returned to the surface at the back of the yacht. She climbed up onto the swimmer's platform and grabbed one of the used air tanks. She dove again in the direction she last saw Kyle.

Aiko reached Kyle and gave him the regulator. After he took a couple of breaths he passed it back to Aiko.

Aiko pointed to the surface and Kyle pointed in the direction toward the skeleton.

Again, they shared the regulator, then dove.

Kyle was holding his side trying to hold back the bleeding. Once they reached the location, Kyle pointed to a piece of stone on the floor of the shelf.

Aiko picked up the rock. Kyle pointed to the skeleton's chest and motioned to break away the extra growth of coral around the bottom of the ribcage.

Aiko took a couple of swings at the coral and eventually broke away enough coral to expose the chest cavity. As they continued to share the regulator, Kyle reached in and waved away a lot of silt that had built up. Then he ran his hand through what was left.

Kyle's hand stopped moving and he and Aiko exchanged a look.

Kyle brought out his closed hand and opened it. There was a handful of sand and silt. Aiko waved her hand across the top layer of silt and as the silt floated away, there in the palm of his hand, was the Monarch Moon.

Near the stern of the SAISHO NO CHI, Aiko breached the surface first and threw the oxygen tank onto the deck of the yacht. As she exited the water, Kyle surfaced, and then she turned to help him out of the water. Kyle had his right elbow tucked in tight to keep pressure on his wound.

Pankov was waiting on the top deck of the yacht where the research vessel had lowered a ramp to gain access to the helm. At the top end of the ramp the armed guards waited.

Pankov helped Aiko at the top of the ladder and she joined him at the helm. Aiko then helped Kyle who was still clutching his right elbow to his side.

"So, where is it?" inquired Pankov.

Kyle looked at Aiko.

Pankov began to pat down across Aiko's body and was getting a little too friendly.

Kyle objected, "She doesn't have it." Kyle knew he needed a distraction and wanted to use the tension between Pankov and Kamiko, "I think Kamiko already has it."

"Why would you say that?" Pankov replied.

"She is an international art dealer. How do you raise the value of something? You reinvent the legend. You yourself told us we can't trust her. Why are you?"

****

Kamiko, with Oksana by her side, was talking to Pankov at the front of the bow of the ship that also doubled as landing area for a helicopter.

Off in the distance a helicopter was approaching.

The seed Kyle had planted in Pankov's mind was getting to him, "You don't seem to be too upset about us not finding the Monarch Moon."

"I guess there is nothing more we can do. That is why I have called for the helicopter."

"And what about Morrell and your daughter?"

Kamiko slapped Pankov hard across the face. As Pankov lowered his head for a moment, Kamiko looked over at her two armed guards, and nodded.

The helicopter was getting close to landing.

Kamiko laid out her new plan, "Stay here. I am taking the girl with me. I will send the helicopter back for you and the luggage."

Kamiko had turned away from the wind created by the rotors but when she turned back to board, two FBI agents in tactical gear had her at gun point. Two more FBI agents exited from the other side of the helicopter and rushed toward Pankov and the guards.

Before the guards could react, they were grabbed from behind by two more FBI agents who had been posing as servants and one of them was Hamamoto, "Lower your weapons! FBI!"

Oksana ran past every one of them and ran into the arms of Aiko and Kyle who were coming down the side passage of the ship.

Half a dozen FBI agents posing as staff aboard the research vessel had taken command of the ship.

Hamamoto got on his radio, "We have command of the ship, Sir."

Hamamoto was on his way to the helipad when Kyle stopped him, "I have to ask you, how did you know our location?"

"One of our drones picked up your frequency."
"What frequency?"

Hamamoto pulled out his cell phone and showed Kyle that he had a program on his phone for tracking. He turned up the volume and the signal was loud and strong. He passed the device near Oksana and it went ballistic. "The flag-pin President Dalton gave to Oksana has the latest nano technology that has a ten-mile radius. If you are within a mile it is accurate within three feet. We had an idea where you might be. After that, it was a matter of time before one of our drones picked up the signal. We had the vessel under surveillance ever since we got the data from the flash drive listing the shell corporations. Our team blended in with the staff and we just had to wait."

He saw Kyle was bleeding, "Let's get you to sick bay."

Inside the ship's sick bay, FBI agent Hamamoto, helped Kyle to a table as Aiko and Oksana remained out in the breezeway.

Hamamoto found a sterile gauze in a drawer and applied it to Kyle's wound, "Let me find one of my other agents who has the medical supplies to come take a look at you."

"Thank you. Have I seen you someplace before? Was it you I saw back at the dock when we acquired the yacht?"

"We've been following your whereabouts ever since you left the states. We had Oksana's signal, then once we saw you leave the compound, we tracked you to the dock. Let me get you some help before you lose too much blood. I'll be right back."

"Can you send in Aiko for a minute please?"

"Sure thing."

Hamamoto left the room and a moment later Aiko and Oksana entered.

Kyle asked Aiko to close the door.

Kyle pulled back the gauze, leaned back a bit, and slipped the end of his finger into his wound. After working his finger deep inside his wound, he was able to pull out a yellow tinted sapphire, about the size of a quarter from its hiding place, "I didn't want to take a chance and have to swallow it like our pirate friend."

"Is that it? Is that the Monarch Moon?"

"Yes, Oksana. It is."

"Can I hold it?" Oksana was so excited to finally see what the mystery was all about.

Aiko took the stone and quickly wiped it clean with a towel and handed it to Oksana. She then handed the towel to Kyle to clean his hands. After doing so, Kyle pressed the gauze back in place.

Kyle had hoped Aiko understood his double meaning, "You saved my life."

"I guess that makes us even."

Aiko leaned in and kissed Kyle.

There was a knock at the door.

Oksana closed her hand around the precious yellow gem as the FBI medic entered.

Kyle was not willing to release Aiko. He raised one finger asking the medic for another minute as he continued to kiss her.

The medic stepped out of the room and closed door.

Oksana opened her hand and was in amazement as she stared at the clarity of the Monarch Moon.

CHAPTER 34

Inside a secured hanger at Dulles Airport, a private plane was standing by.

President Dalton was escorted by four Secret Service agents who were all wearing sunglasses, that is, all but the one who was alongside the President.

He gave them a nod as he approached Kamiko, who was escorted by two FBI agents, one of them being, Rick Hamamoto. Next to them was Pankov who was also book-ended and by two FBI agents.

Off to one side were Kyle, Aiko, and Oksana.

Dalton pulled aside one of his agents, "I want two F-15's ready to launch on my order."

The agent confirmed his order, "Yes, Sir."

Dalton walked up to Kamiko and gave her a message, "Your daughter, Aiko, wanted one last chance to see you and give you a message."

Kamiko looked over Dalton's shoulder at Aiko. Aiko reached in the top of her blouse and pulled out a pendent that was hanging from her necklace. It was the Monarch Moon.

Kamiko tried to hold in her rage but her eyes gave her away. Dalton saw this and by the time he turned around, Aiko had hidden the stone back inside the collar of her blouse.

Dalton turned back to Kamiko, "I guess we're all done here." Dalton then leaned in close to Kamiko so she was the only one who could hear, "Except for the part where you're going a way for a very long time."

Kamiko spoke back in a very low tone as well, "We are not done. You think Oksana is your only dirty little secret?"

The Secret Service agent standing next to Dalton took a phone call on a secure cell phone and reached it out to Dalton, "Sir, it's your wife. She says it urgent."

Kamiko's smile held a secret, "You had better take that."

Dalton took the call, "Jillian? Is everything alright?" All Dalton could do was listen as Jillian's words sent his mind into a tailspin.

Dalton hung up the phone.

Kamiko's intonation let Dalton know she knew the meaning in every word Jillian had to beg her husband to listen to, "Yes, I have spoken to your wife. Not only did I confirm that Oksana is your daughter but I also sent her copies of the photos of you and Karina from the Vintage Hotel when you were just an up and coming Senator. We both agreed it would be in everyone's best interest that those pictures never saw the light of day. An illegitimate daughter is one thing, but with a Russian whore is another."

Dalton grabbed Kamiko firmly by the throat.

Kamiko just smiled.

Just as the Secret Service agent stepped in, Dalton let her go.

Kamiko caught her breath and calmly resumed, "If we are not airborne in ten minutes, not only will those pictures be leaked to the press, but you will go down as the President who let hundreds of people die for no reason."

"What have you done?"

One of Dalton's Secret Service agents approached, "Sir, we have to go. We have a live threat."

The President's limo was standing by.

Dalton turned to Kamiko, "This wasn't part of the deal!"

"In about nine minutes, there are going to be a lot of unhappy passengers waiting for all of these planes to be sniffed out one at a time."

"Which plane?"

"I will identify the plane when I am airborne. Eight minutes."

The Secret Service agent held one of his hands to his ear bud, "Sir, we now have a second threat."

Dalton wanted to rip out Kamiko's throat, "How many?"

Dalton only saw the worst in humanity as he looked into the eyes of a woman who had no soul. As leader of the free world, Dalton never felt so helpless.

Kamiko drove in the final nail, "I own you."

Dalton gave the order, "Let her go."

A Secret Service agent wasn't sure if he had heard him right, "Sir?"

"You heard me. Let her go."

Kamiko held her cool knowing she was holding all of the cards. All but one.

"Just so we know what is at stake, I am going to have to have an insurance marker."

Kamiko looked over at Oksana.

Dalton responded with a resounding, "No!"

"Do you want to have to explain to your daughter when she sees pictures of her father, the President of the United States, tied to a bed with her now dead mother on the covers of the tabloids? Or, would you rather have to explain to the American public and to the passenger's families how you chose your little red butterfly over them? Either way, you lose."

Dalton walked over to Kyle, Aiko, and Oksana. Dalton placed his hand on Oksana's shoulder and turned to Aiko, "I'm sorry."

Dalton led Oksana over toward Kamiko as Aiko and Kyle stepped forward but were immediately stopped and held back by Secret Service agents.

Dalton stopped and knelt down in front of Oksana, "I need you to know, I will be doing everything in my power to keep you safe and this will be all over soon."

Dalton then gave Oksana a fatherly hug for the first time.

Oksana felt his compassion, "I trust you…"

Oksana then stepped back, "And I trust you, Mr. President."

Dalton was so touched he could hardly stand it. He then led Oksana over to Kamiko.

Kamiko didn't waste any time. She led Oksana up the stairs and Pankov was right on their heels as they all boarded the jet.

The jet carrying Kamiko, Pankov, and Oksana taxied away from the hanger, crossed over in front of a second set of private hangers, and made its way down to the end of the runway. A couple of minutes later, it reappeared as it stopped and held at the end of the runway for clearance.

Kyle and Aiko approached Dalton.

"What's going on?" Kyle asked, "Where are they taking Oksana?"

Before Dalton could answer one of his agents stepped in, "It's a security issue and we're going to have to leave it at that."

Dalton waved off his agent who then backed away. Dalton had to close off his feelings as a father and answer as a President. He took a cell phone out of his pocket and turned on the same app Hamamoto had showed Kyle on the yacht, "I can't go into the security details but we have the ability to track Oksana."

Kyle saw the app and he could tell from the read-out that Oksana's signal was strong and only about one-hundred yards away.

The Secret Service agent stepped back in, "Sir, they have clearance."

Dalton addressed his agents, "Scramble two fighters. Once we have those planes identified, if their jet deviates off course, give the order."

"Yes, Sir."

The roar of Kamiko's jet's engines coming up to full throttle echoed loudly from the end of the nearby runway.

Kyle felt his heart drop and had to yell over the noise, "What order is that?"

Dalton didn't give him an answer. Everyone turned and watched as the Marine Science Technologies jet rushed down the tarmac, and within seconds, was up to speed and the jet was on its way.

Kyle turned back to Dalton, "How could you?"

"I didn't have a choice," Dalton held up the tracker. "But we already have jets in the air to track her."

Kyle saw something on the tracker that no one else had noticed yet. The dot that represented Oksana was still one-hundred yards away. Kyle grabbed Aiko by the hand and began running out of the hanger toward the end of the runway.

"Kyle, what is going on?"

Kyle ran as fast as Aiko could keep up, "They got off the plane!"

CHAPTER 35

Inside the private hanger nearest the end of the runway, Victor opened the back door of a waiting limousine and gestured for Oksana to get in. As much as Oksana wanted to stay strong for Aiko, she couldn't help but feel like the last domino. Once inside the limousine Victor removed a bottle of vodka that had been chilling in a bucket of ice and poured himself a drink. It reminded Oksana of being alone and sitting across from Marcus as she saw the darkest side of man. The way he looked at her just before he took what he paid for, her innocence.

Victor took another sip of his drink as he looked at Oksana, not as a little girl he raised, but as the young woman she was becoming, "Do you like exotic animals?"

"Where are you taking me?"

"To your new home."

For a moment, in her mind, Oksana tried to find that place in her heart that she truly could call home. After all, her mother was dead and her father, the President, just had to make a calculated choice of her one day helping to save his own life over that of a plane full of people. He chose the politically correct choice over family.

Victor's voice brought her out of the fog, "We have our own little island that comes with no extradition. It was once a state-of-the-art government research facility that comes with a private beach five miles long."

"You sold me to that man for $40,000. Why?"

"For the right price, everything is for sale. It's what I do and soon you'll be worth five times that much."

Oksana felt a sense of worth kick in that Aiko had instilled in her and that's just what she did, she kicked. Oksana felt the control come over her body and with catlike reflexes she kicked the drink right out of Victor's hand. As the glass caromed off the side wall of limousine, its contents splashed all over Victor, then the glass itself smashed into the minibar, breaking the vodka bottle in half. Victor, without hesitation, backhanded Oksana so hard that she lost all sense of time and direction. She sat there, momentarily stunned.

Kamiko had been on a private satellite phone confirming the rest of her plans of the misdirection, "Are the accommodations ready?"

Victor and Oksana were close enough for him to hear the dim reply of a woman's voice over the sat phone say, "Yes, we are standing by for departure."

Victor thought he recognized the barely audible voice, "Was that, Birgitta?"

"Yes. Ms. Bogdanoff has been put in charge of our advance team on the island."

"What would Karl think of his daughter now working for you?"

"You would think he would be grateful."

At the opposite end of the hanger, one of the standard sized metal side doors opened, and two men wearing ill fitted airport mechanic overalls entered the hanger. Each man was carrying a red metal toolbox. Once inside, they walked over to a nearby portable bench that had been set up near the front of the single engine 2000 Piper Malibu Mirage, and began unlatching their tool boxes.

They each pulled off the top tray, set them to the side, and removed silenced Berettas from the bottom of their tool boxes.

Just as each man had made sure the slides of their weapons were in working order and they each had a full clip, a security guard entered through the front open side of the hanger. Before the guard's eyes could adjust from the bright sunlight, he was dead.

One of the would-be mechanics trained his weapon on the front door as the other took care of the body by dragging it across the cement floor to a nearby work bench. The assassin picked up the body, placed it in a desk chair, and rolled it up to the edge of the bench. He then arranged the corpse's crossed arms on the bench and then placed the man's head on his arms giving him the appearance he was sleeping.

This distraction worked in Kyle's and Aiko's favor as they were able to slip in the back door and take a hiding place nearby, behind two 55 gallon drums.

Kamiko folded up the sat phone and handed it to Victor, "We don't have much time. Get the girl in the car. I want to make sure we are not followed." Kamiko headed across the hanger to talk to the two assassins dressed as airport mechanics.

From behind the 55 gallon drums, Kyle and Aiko heard the heels of Kamiko's dress shoes on the cement floor getting louder the closer as she got to their hiding place. Kyle estimated she was within about 20 feet before he sensed she had altered her direction toward the front of the plane where the hired gunmen were waiting for their instructions.

Oksana looked through the tinted window of the limousine across the hanger and saw Kamiko reach into her purse, remove two small manila envelopes and handed each one of the men their cash payments.

Kamiko gave them a final order, "I do not want any more surprises, gentlemen."

Victor hit the interior switch in the ceiling of the limousine and opened the sunroof. He stood up through the open gap in the roof and saw that Kamiko was approaching the limousine.

Kamiko stopped suddenly as she saw the frozen look on Victor's face. She turned around just in time to see four Secret Service agents with weapons drawn enter the far end of the hanger.

The first two agents went down taking multiple rounds, their bullet proof vests taking most of the punishment from the silenced Berettas of the disguised assassins. Dozens of shots were exchanged in both directions as the agents took cover.

Kamiko saw a silhouette appear by the back door from behind the 55 gallon drums. She watched as Kyle, in a full-on sprint, came in behind the two assassins throwing his legs out in front of him, and with a hard slide took out the legs of one of them and reached out his arms to grab the legs of the other, taking them both off their feet.

One of the men lost his gun as his head connected with the cement floor with a thud. The man's body laid dazed with his back to Kyle. Kyle grabbed the man's Beretta then grabbed the assassin from behind, putting him in a choke hold. He used him as a shield as he fired two rounds, center mass, into the second assassin, killing him instantly. Kyle then turned the tip of the silencer into the chest of his human shield and squeezed off two more rounds.

Kyle felt a sharp pain in his left side as one of the rounds passed through the assassin's chest and on its way out grazed one of his ribs.

Kyle rolled the dead man's body to the side just as Aiko came to his aide. She helped Kyle get to his feet then retrieved the second gun from the would-be assassin.

Kamiko extended her hand toward Victor, "Give me the phone. Are the numbers set?"

"Yes. They're ready to go."

Kamiko turned around and saw Aiko and Kyle had taken out both of her hired guns. She raised her hand holding the pre-programmed cell phone high in the air for everyone to see. Kyle saw the Secret Service agents coming up on their six and waved them off asking them to hold back.

Inside the limousine, Oksana had regained her senses, and could see that Kyle had a gun in each hand. The closer they got, Oksana watched as Kyle slowly raised both guns out in front of him and had one trained on Victor and one on Kamiko.

Kamiko responded by prominently holding the cell phone out in front of her with her thumb hovering over the send button.

Kyle and Aiko stopped far enough back so Kyle could also keep an eye on the driver of the limousine as he sat behind the wheel. Kyle momentarily took his gun off Victor and pointed it at the driver and gestured with the tip of the silencer. The driver got the message and placed his hands on the wheel at 10 and 2.

While the focus was off him, Victor kept his eyes on Kyle as he slowly reached down to remove his gun from the holster in the small of his back.

Inside the limousine, Oksana quietly removed the top half of the broken vodka bottle from the ice bucket. Victor held the gun down along his side and slowly clicked off the safety.

Outside the limo Oksana could hear Kyle's plea, "All we want is Oksana."

Kamiko's reply was meant to send a message, "She is not yours to demand, and never was."

Oksana knew when she heard Kyle's response that in fact she did have a home to go to, "You're wrong."

Oksana felt the love Kyle had for her and Aiko as one, as family.

While the driver of the limousine was looking in Kyle's direction, he could see out of the corner of his eye through the car's partition, that Victor had drawn his gun. The driver, hoping to cause a distraction, started to slide his hand down from the 2 o'clock position.

The movement in the front of the limousine did catch Kyle's attention. Kyle once again took the gun off of Victor and motioned for the driver put his hand back.

Victor took this moment to slowly start to raise his gun up.

Oksana gripped the neck of the broken vodka bottle like a handle, and with all her might, thrust the sharp, jagged end of the bottle up into Victor's groin area. Blood instantly began draining out of the bottle neck onto Oksana's wrist and arm as the glass had severed the artery in Victor's thigh.

The instant pain caused Victor's body to flinch and tighten up, causing him to raise his arm out of the limo which exposed him holding the gun. The pain Victor had felt was gone. The bullet from Kyle's gun that entered the center of his forehead took care of that.

His limp body fell back into the limo.

Everyone was calm except for Oksana and she screamed and climbed out the far side of the limousine.

Kamiko and Kyle were at a standoff as Kamiko still had her thumb over the phone and Kyle now had both guns on her.

Kyle knew the threat Kamiko held in her hand was real. He thought to himself, she was way too calm. The doors on the far side of the hanger opened. Two Secret Service men entered followed by the President. As they made their way across the hanger, the President could see the standoff happening in front of him.

He could see Oksana had made her way to the back of the limo as Aiko raised her hand and motioned for her to stay there. The President told his men to back down.

The driver of the limousine stepped out of the car using the car as a shield, raised his hand, and showed everyone he too was holding a phone with his thumb over the send button. Kamiko knew she didn't quite hold all the cards but she held enough, "My driver and I are going to leave now and I suggest no one follows."

One of the Secret Service agents took a few steps in to get a better angle on the driver.

Kamiko pointed toward the agent who instantly stopped in his tracks, "This one is on you." Then she pointed at her driver who in turn pressed the button on his phone.

Off in the distance a loud explosion reverberated across the tarmac and shook the building. A 747 at United Airlines gate 14 was no longer. The plane had exploded and was now engulfed in flames.

Kamiko showed everyone she had her hand on her phone ready to press her send button at will. Kyle and Aiko watched as the driver dialed up another number on his cell phone. Kyle got the message and motioned everyone to stay back.

A Secret Service agent took a phone call and let the President know, "Sir, the plane was empty."

"How many planes do we have left to de-board?"

"It's hard to say, Sir. We're in the process now."

Kamiko had everyone's attention, "Time to go. Who knows how many will be on board the next?"

The driver moved down to the passenger door on the opposite side of the car and removed Victor's body and left it to bleed out on the cold slab of the cement floor of the hanger. The driver then got back in behind the wheel and using the button in his door, lowered the back-side passenger window.

Kamiko climbed into the back of limousine. After closing the door, she stuck her phone out the window and showed everyone the phone as she gestured to the driver to go. As he put the car in gear, Oksana ran from the back of the car into the safety of Aiko's arms.

As the limousine made its way clear of the hanger, everyone walked out into the open to see the limousine drive off toward the exit gate.

One of the Secret Service agents asked, "Mr. President, would you like me to have them detained at the exit gate?"

Dalton watched as Kamiko pulled her arm into the limo and raised the window.

He could see the smoke from the burning plane that was in pieces at the departure gate and the smell of the gas and burning rubber from the explosion. It left a bad taste in his mouth. He couldn't risk the chance of an additional device taking out another plane full of people. In a shallow breath he replied, "No. Let them go."

The Secret Service agent noticed the President seemed to be out of breath, "Are you alright, Sir?"

"I'll be fine."

Dalton wasn't fine. For days now, he had been hiding the fact the night sweats had been getting worse, he had begun to lose weight, and the headaches were becoming more frequent.

Dalton did his best to hide his pain as he asked his Secret Service detail, "Can you bring my car around? I'd like to give my daughter a ride in it onto the tarmac to Air Force One."

"Yes, Sir. Right away."

Kyle, Aiko, and Oksana walked up to the President.

Dalton could see all that Oksana had been through.

Her clothes on her right side were spattered with blood, where her right arm had brushed up against her side. One side of her face was red and a bruise was forming from where Victor had backhanded her. One thing he didn't see, was fear.

"Are you all right Oksana?"

Oksana looked at Kyle and Aiko, "I will be."

"How would you like to fly home with me on Air Force One?"

Aiko spoke for the three of them, "It would be an honor Sir."

"Good, because I would like to talk to you, Kyle, about heading up a task force."

"What kind of task force, Sir?"

"We have hundreds of girls out there with tracking devices in them and we're going to need a team to locate them and take down the buyers. We already have substantial funding in place for the project. Our guys were able to hack a couple of the Masato Enterprises foreign accounts. All we need now is a team leader."

Kyle had no words other than, "Can I have some time to think about it?"

The President replied, "The position is yours but I will need an answer soon. Every day, those girls are losing hope that someday, someone, just might be there to rescue them. Why can't that be you?"

Just as the President's limo was driving up, Dalton reached out his hand to Oksana and she took it. They began to walk toward the limo. In turn, Kyle took Aiko's hand and followed.

****

President Dalton was sitting in his chair behind the Resolute desk in the Oval Office looking out the window at his wife, Jillian, as she was on the lawn playing with the dog. Watching Jillian, he had to wonder about the woman who for all these years knew him not as the President of the United Stated but as Spencer, the man who changed their world. Now the past he had kept hidden from her has been exposed. That world, their lives, would never be the same.

There was a knock at the door.

Director Wintersteen entered, "Sir, we have confirmation, there were two more bombs located on separate flights and they have been defused according to instructions that we received from Kamiko Masato. It's been a real mess but air travel has resumed at Dulles." Wintersteen waited for a reply but did not get one, "Sir?"

"Yes, what is it?"

"Dr. Riggs would like to know if you can come and see him as soon as possible regarding your last check-up. What can I tell him is a good time for you?"

Dalton continued to look out the window.
Wintersteen waited a moment, then asked, "Sir, what would you like to do?"

Dalton again had no words and just motioned with his hand with a slight backhand wave. Wintersteen took his cue and left the commander-in-chief alone in his office.

CHAPTER 36

Being back at the seaside beach house was a welcome feeling but this time it was different. Kyle knew what he and Aiko had was real and having Oksana with them made it feel all the more natural. Everything they had been through had brought them closer together, more than ever.

Yes, he knew things would be different. That was evident as he was doing the cooking. Not that he didn't know how to cook but what he was making was his own version of Sukiyaki.

After the stir-fry was ready, Kyle brought the pan over to the table and offered the chicken and vegetable dish right out of the pan. He served everyone a portion and of course a double portion for himself.

Kyle took his seat and realized when Oksana had set the table she had only given him a set of chopsticks. Aiko picked up her set of chopsticks and started to eat. Oksana did the same. Kyle shook his head and knew he was out numbered and would give it a shot.

It took a few attempts at failing before Kyle finally had to give in, "Okay, how do you work these things?"

Oksana got up and went to his side with her chopsticks in hand to show him how to hold his chopsticks properly.

With a little encouragement from Aiko he finally was getting the hang of it and Aiko and Oksana cheered when he finally got a piece of chicken to his mouth on the first try.

After dinner, Kyle was sitting on the couch looking at a legal-size envelope postmark from Washington, D.C., as Oksana was playing with the dominos on the coffee table in front of them.

Aiko sat down next to Kyle and asked, "Are you going to open it?"

Kyle had been toying with the idea of the task force ever sense President Dalton had brought it up to him, "We've already talked about this and you know, if I open this, there could be no going back."

"I'm afraid there is no going back, only forward," Aiko responded.

Kyle opened the envelope and it contained a letter outlining the task force and a check for $500,000. Kyle thought about it for a moment, "Are you sure about this? If we go down this road, the next time we cross paths with Kamiko, there's no stopping until its done."

"We will take this journey together and I trust you with my life."

There was nothing more to say, Kyle and Aiko understood they were family now, and would do anything and everything to protect it.

Oksana took the silence as it was her turn to ask a question, "So, how much is the check?"

"Never you mind," Kyle replied as he folded up the paperwork and stuffed it back into the envelope.

To change the subject, Kyle began helping Oksana finish setting up the dominoes. Once they had them all set up Aiko asked, "Which one are you?"

Immediately Oksana picked up the first domino, "This one." She put the domino back in place, tipped it over, and the rest of the dominos followed.

Aiko was very proud of Oksana, "I can see you are becoming my own little shadow warrior."

Kyle wanted to know more, "What is a shadow warrior?"

"The sensei who trained me how to use the katana used to call me his little Shadow Warrior. He said I was the best student he ever trained because I fought so hard trying change my past, he thought I was trying to release my shadow."

"What does that mean?" asked Oksana.

"He was saying, no matter how hard I fought, my shadow would always be there and to survive I would have to come to peace with that."

"I think you have, Aiko." Kyle replied.

"I am afraid there is a lot about me you do not know that will frighten you."

"I don't know how that could be. I love everything about you and if ever the past tries to take the place of our future, I'll always be there for you. Right here."

Kyle leaned in and gave Aiko a kiss.

Aiko began to let go and believe. The words just came to her and without holding back she just let them out as if the truth would follow like a shadow, "I love you, Kyle Morrell."

After hearing Aiko say the words he longed to hear from her for so long, he kissed her gently once again.

Aiko and Kyle both noticed that Oksana was exhausted and encouraged her to go to bed. Oksana didn't bother putting away the dominos and got up and gave Aiko a hug, "I love you. Good night, Aiko." She then turned and paused before giving Kyle a hug, "Yeah, I love you, too."

Kyle gave her a gentle hug letting her know she too was loved, "Good night, Oksana."

As Oksana walked away, Kyle could see Aiko was very emotional, "Are you okay?"

"Yes. I just need a moment."

"Okay. I'll lock up. Take your time."

"Thank you. I'll join you in a minute."

Once Kyle had made sure the house was safe he headed to the master bedroom.

Aiko took a moment to stop next to the sword display stand. All three swords were there. The katana, known as The Guardian was in the top slot. The wakizashi was in the lower slot and lying in the open drawer, was the tanto.

Aiko removed the necklace from around her neck. She held the Monarch Moon up to a nearby light and saw the amber glow from it on the wall nearby.

Inside the amber glow was a perfectly cut and balanced projection of what appeared to be a monarch butterfly encircled in a yellow moon.

Aiko turned off the light and in the glow from the full moon outside, she placed the stone in the drawer with the tanto, closed it, and reversed the dials locking the drawer.

The emotions that Aiko was feeling were like none she had ever felt. A sense of family and all that came with it. The responsibility for Oksana, the love that was growing between her and Kyle, and for the love she had inside her. Aiko put both her hands on her lower belly, "Hai, Kyle-son, watashitachi wa imaya kazokudesu. We are truly a family now."

Made in the USA
Lexington, KY
30 July 2017